I0831857

HEART STONE

LEGENDS OF THE FALLEN BOOK 8

J.A. CULICAN

H.M. GOODEN

Paperback ISBN: 978-1-692127-33-6

Hardback ISBN: 978-1-949621-14-3

Audra
Desert of Souls
Bor'sur
Western March
Lower City
The Oubilee Desert
Blasted Lands
Bomrega Island
Prison
Dragon Dominion
Barren Wastes
Arrecem Secer
The Library
Cliffside
Caera
Low Forest (humans)
Low Forest (elves)
Great River Gethaurelle
Rilyo
Waterdeep
Bruhier
Lamruil
Thimmel
Southern Plains
Barepost
Havenport
Gleet
Lynia

CHAPTER 1

I sat looking over the bow of the airship, trying to calm my breathing after the excitement of the previous few hours.

We'd been incredibly lucky to return from the temple as Captain Baeley was apologizing to the dockmaster and backing toward the ship, ready to depart without us.

While she'd managed to buy us some time, she'd finally worn out her welcome about the time we'd slipped onto the back of the ship. When she'd caught our movement, she snapped straight up and gave the dockmaster an obsequious smile, the cajoling tone turning into a cheery goodbye.

I'd noticed his confused look at her abrupt about-face as we slunk below deck, but his satisfaction at getting his way had replaced it almost immediately.

And that was why, barely five minutes later, we were back on Captain Baeley's airship, watching Bomrega Island disappear in the distance as we headed back to Starside, our mission complete.

My bag weighed heavily around my neck and shoulder, and I absently flipped it to my lap.

It was large enough to carry not only my notebook and

writing stylus, but also the books I'd borrowed from the Library at Abrecem Secer, the paper Jarid had given me, and now, most importantly, the goblet I'd won from the magical orb inside the temple.

It was the goblet which drew my attention now.

I opened my satchel, drawing it out to examine it now I was in the safety of the ship. It was an average sized cup, suitable for a banquet, and on initial inspection appeared to be an ordinary, albeit pretty, item. I held the goblet, feeling its bronzed and ornately carved surface warm in a way metal shouldn't. The same way the key from the Library had warmed when I'd entered the room. They were similar, acting in a way I'd never seen before.

In the temple on Bomrega, I hadn't even been certain what I was looking for. I'd merely been following a series of symbols I'd discovered in the Library, in a textbook Jarid wasn't supposed to show me in the first place. I'd followed the symbols all the way to a hidden room, which no one had been in before. This had angered and frightened Luban, the head Librarian, enough he'd posted guards and Jarid had expressed fear his job was no longer secure.

The goblet itself wasn't in any of the texts I'd researched, and I still wasn't sure if the cup was a reward or punishment. The Library had been cryptic so far, and even now, safe on the flying ship racing away from the lawless, dragon clan ruled island, the images the orb had shared with me were disturbing. Scenes of my friends fighting and dying, the feeling deep within me all of this was possible. Knowing if I couldn't solve this problem, I would go down fighting as well.

I'd learned something about myself I hadn't expected to today. I'd always thought myself a scholar, an elf of wisdom and learning. I'd always felt constricted by the bounds of my nobility and the idea I was good for nothing except an advantageous marriage. I had never thought of becoming a warrior in anything other than abstract terms, or perhaps a way to get out of my duties to marry.

At least, not since my teen years when Father had firmly halted the notion I was to follow in my brother's footsteps.

The orb had shown me a different side. My inner drive to fight was there and shone as strongly as the Librarian within. The idea I was a warrior as much as a scholar was confounding yet had a rightness and filled something I hadn't known was missing until I'd met its challenge. Somehow, I felt I was now complete, and marveled at what my quest for knowledge had brought.

I turned the goblet over in my hands, the metal still slightly warm at my touch and had a sudden realization. I knew what our next step was. Excitement bubbled inside me. I stood, placing the goblet in my satchel, and headed to find my friends.

I found Will first, standing near the stern with Captain Baeley. I couldn't hear what they were saying from where I was but given the recent events, I imagined he was filling her in.

She'd been casting surreptitious glances at me as I approached while he talked, and I nodded my head once before turning to look for the others.

Sel had taken up a perch on the side near where they were conversing, leaning over to watch the scenery fly by as he had on our way to the island.

I watched him, not even trying to suppress a smile at his excitement. I couldn't help thinking how much he'd grown and changed during our trip. I'd always known he carried a spark of adventure inside. His wondering spirit had become obvious with every new bump in the road to find the goblet.

He'd risen to each obstacle with a grace above his age and had impressed me.

At first, I feared he would die following me out of his sense of duty. He was my servant, after all. But watching his character mold under hardship, I'd quickly understood he was helping me for the same reason I was on my quest in the first place. To do something good and stop the evil spreading through our world.

My guilty conscience eased somewhat as I acknowledged that fact, even though, if anything happened to him, I'd still feel responsible.

Gwen was nowhere to be seen on deck. Deciding to check on her before bothering the others, who seemed content where they were, I headed below deck to find her exactly where I thought I would; curled up with her wolves.

I paused to watch them. They weren't sleeping, but I had no idea what was passing between the four of them. I could tell she was communicating with them in her own way as they stared at each other calmly, as if they were somewhere different than the small bunk room.

Sometimes, I felt Gwen was more wolf than elf, which didn't bother me the way it should have, or the way it bothered the other elves in the Low Forest, which had led to her living alone in a treehouse outside of town. Our relationship had changed as well, strengthened, becoming something more than mere friendship during our journey, even if I didn't have the words to describe it.

I stepped onto a board which creaked loudly, announcing my presence.

She looked up, untangling herself as she slid into a sitting position on the bunk and tilted her head. "Everything okay?" She seemed to be searching my face for trouble, so I smiled brightly to reassure her, which seemed to work as her shoulders relaxed and she leaned back against Swift.

"Yes, everything's fine. But I've been thinking…" I stepped closer, pausing when the wolves shifted their attention from her to me.

She raised an eyebrow and before I could protest, the

wolves jumped onto the floor, curling back up in a cozy puddle next to the bunk.

"Thinking? I'm not entirely sure that's a good thing where you're concerned." She half-groaned, half-laughed as her deep forest green eyes twinkled with humor.

I chuckled, sitting beside her on the bunk. "True, thinking does seem to have gotten us into a few scrapes. But now that I have the goblet, I think we need to go back to the Library."

She flung an arm around my shoulders as she shot me a rueful smile.

The action sent a warm wave of contentment coursing through me. It was so nice to have a friend like her.

"I thought as much. I mean, what's a Librarian going to do but head back to the Library once their quest is over?"

"That's just the thing. I don't think our quest is over. In fact, I'm positive this is just the first piece of the puzzle. I know extremely little about the goblet I found. I'm sure it's important to trapping Dag'draath and stopping his legions of darkness once and for all, but not how." I rose abruptly, feeling restless. As I paced across the tiny space, the wolves tracked me with their eyes, causing me to feel even more out of sorts. How could I impress how uncertain I was without appearing afraid?

"My findings in the Library have led me this far, but they never mentioned a goblet. I didn't even have an inkling there was one involved until the room right before the strange globe with the magic energy where I found it. And getting to that room was even harder than making it through the challenges the Library set for me. I mean, if it hadn't been for an old spell I've known since I was small, I probably wouldn't have made it past the first room."

She narrowed her eyes, tilting her head to the side as she examined me with an unusual thoroughness. "Interesting. You never mentioned you had magic before."

I brushed her observation aside, uncomfortable with her

inspection. "I don't, not really. I mean, I've never spent much time developing it. My sister, Cassiopeia, is the one who's skilled in that department. I never thought it would be of much use in my daily life, and once I discovered books I had even less interest in magic, other than learning about it from a scholarly perspective."

She raised her eyebrows. "Perhaps these tests are trying to tell you something."

I dropped my chin, crossing my arms across my chest as if doing so would protect me from the worry filling me.

"I know. Everything so far seems to have been designed to test me, to stretch me beyond what I think I'm possible of accomplishing. I've learned things frankly I wouldn't have believed I was capable of before I was forced into the situation."

"Like the time you developed amazing and impossible fighting skills out of nowhere, taking down a giant slaver both a trained soldier and I were unable to beat with our far greater combat experience?"

I grimaced, still unable to understand how it had been possible for an untrained bookworm to take down a scarred and ruthless human without an arsenal at my disposal. "Yeah. Not to mention the fact Kramson gave me a key to the library." I lifted it out of my shirt, moving closer to show her.

Her eyes widened.

I couldn't remember if I'd shown it to her before, but since my adventure in the temple, it had glowed with a warmth I was sure would be visible to others if I took it out of my shirt, which I hadn't done before now.

"When did it start doing that?" She held her hand out hesitantly, pulling back at the last moment before touching it with her fingers.

"It started in the temple. It was important in conjunction with the vase. I'm not sure I would've made it to the final test if

I hadn't put the two items together, but I've got no idea how I knew to do that."

I leaned forward, my nose almost touching hers as I confided in her. It was hard to say the next part out loud. "The strangest thing about it all was I could almost hear something telling me what to do. There's no way I should have been able to recognize the vase was important in the first place. It was the plainest thing in the room."

She exhaled, a light puff of air which stirred the hair beside my face. "It's obvious whatever's happening is something you were meant to be a part of."

Her eyes clouded, taking on a faraway look for several seconds before they sharpened and looked at me intently again. "You know I sometimes see things. Perhaps I don't understand what I see as well as Loglan and the centaurs do, but I know we have the potential to stop another Dark War if we work together. I think something, a being out there, maybe even a god we don't yet know or understand, wants you to succeed. I think it's why we've been doing the things we have, even when nothing about it makes sense."

As I considered her words, the same inner restlessness caused me to begin pacing again. After a few moments of exertion, I stopped and regarded her, a temporary calm replacing my anxiety.

"I think you're right. I think there's something, or someone, there who is laying the steps. I want to find out who and why."

We looked at each other. I couldn't tell what she was thinking so I was surprised when she stood and gave me a hug. My arms reflexively went around her and for a moment, I enjoyed the warmth and peace of the unexpected embrace. My heart swelled as I realized again just how lucky I was to have her in my life.

"Hey, am I interrupting something? I can come back later, if you prefer."

I let go, whirling to see Will leaning in the doorway, one leg loosely crossed over the other as he twirled a piece of grass in his mouth.

Where had he gotten grass on a flying ship? I shook my head at the randomness and brought my attention back to his question.

"Nope. I was just saying we have to go back to the Library at Abrecem Secer. I need to get back into the Suun Room to find out why the goblet is important."

He walked into the room, nodding his head thoughtfully.

Sel appeared behind him and I smiled, including him in my next statement. "I'm certain the goblet is just the first item we have to find. I'm not as sure my plan will work, but one thing I learned in the temple was regardless of how much success I have, at least if I keep using the resources in the Library, I'm not giving up. One way or another, I plan to fight the darkness trying to take over Lynia to the end. I'd love to have you all with me along the journey, but I'll understand if things don't work out."

I cleared my throat, my voice becoming oddly thick as I remembered the visions I'd received from the orb. "It's meant a lot to me, your support thus far."

I looked at everyone, but my eyes rested longest on Sel as I tried to impress my appreciation to him.

He nodded, pressing his lips together as he silently acknowledged my gratitude. Growing up as a slave in Cliffside, I was sure thanks weren't something he'd heard often from his elven masters before we'd met. While our relationship had never been strictly master and servant, it was only recently his demeanor had thawed and become more relaxed with me, allowing him to treat me as a friend.

"Thank you, Rhin." His quiet words solidified my impression. In the past, he would have never addressed me by name in front of others, especially another elf, and hardly ever used it in private. It made me happier than I'd expected.

I smiled and was about to speak again when Will blew a raspberry.

"Yeah, yeah. Enough of this touchy-feely stuff. I had a feeling you might say such a thing, so I took the liberty when I was recounting our little adventure to Captain Baeley of instructing her to return to Starside and the Library. I hope I did good?" He raised an eyebrow as he watched me.

I nodded, knowing the abrupt subject change was his way of dismissing the uncomfortably sentimental moment.

He may have dismissed my thanks, but he sounded a smidge less sarcastic. He could pretend otherwise, but his actions showed me his sense of unity was as strong as mine.

We lapsed into a companionable silence, going our own ways until the ship docked in Starside.

The guys went above deck to watch the flight, and I curled up to do more research while Gwen napped with the wolves.

Sooner than I realized, we were back to Starside and thanking the captain and her crew for their service.

Will promised to pay her extra for her trouble the next time he saw her, and we headed back to the Library.

WITH THE WOLVES not allowed inside and the memory of the incident with the slaver still fresh in all our minds, I reluctantly said goodbye to them once we were safely at the Library.

"Be safe, okay? I'm worried about you being alone in a strange city."

She raised an eyebrow, looking down at her wolves. "You know I'm never alone."

I growled in irritation and crossed my arms. "Fine, I'm worried when you're not with me. If anything happens to you, I won't know about it until it's too late. It makes me uncomfortable."

"I can take her to the outskirts of the city." He looked at

Gwen and her wolves, "I'll help you set up camp. I know a relatively quiet area."

She looked at me. "Does that help?"

"I guess so. I'll try to be quick and join you soon. Be careful."

Smiling, she gave me a tight squeeze.

I wished I could protect her with more than just a fervent prayer as we hugged. When I pulled away, I had to press my lips together to hold back more motherly admonitions I knew she wouldn't appreciate.

Will tossed me a jaunty salute, skipping down the stairs without a backward glance.

I watched for a moment as the small entourage descended the long marble steps, then turned and headed inside the Library with my faithful shadow.

"What? You again?" The gruff sound of Kramson's disgruntled voice greeted me the second I walked into the Library.

I smiled as brightly as I could but could tell from his expression, he wasn't any more excited to see me than Luban would have been. To his credit he didn't try to shoo or hurt me, which was kind.

"I need more information. I was hoping to return to my previous books."

Kramson narrowed his eyes, causing them to look like small slits in his round face. "As the Library has, for some unknown reason, seen fit to gift you with the privileges of a Librarian, I can hardly stop you. I will, however, insist you keep an apprentice with you at all times."

He watched me reprovingly, folding his arms across his rounded stomach. I knew he was referring to when I'd left Jarid behind and snuck off to follow the symbols.

With a delicate incline of my head, I thanked him. "Absolutely. Help would be much appreciated. Shall I wait here for him?"

Kramson nodded abruptly before disappearing, his long brown robes swishing behind him like an angry cat. I sat in one of the ornately decorated chairs in the lobby while Sel stood silently at my side.

This version of the Library was decorated almost identically to the entrance in Sunland, apart from a beautiful mural depicting a magical starry night sky on the ceiling instead of the open sunroof in the center. I lost myself in the picture and blinked to find Jarid standing beside me.

His face was solemn, but his eyes twinkled, even as Kramson glared daggers at both of us.

"Do a better job this time." Kramson practically threw the words, including him in the glare I'd previously thought special and reserved only for me. "I recommend you avoid anything out of the usual this time."

He gave the Librarian a deep bow, straightening after a respectful interval. "We shall be extremely proper. I'd hate for Luban to become any angrier with me."

Kramson gave him another suspicious look, before turning on his heel and stomping away.

When Jarid bowed to me, his lips curled into a smile. "Thank you for your return business. Where would you like to go?" His words were bland and generic, but his eyes had a warning in them.

I knew any request could be overheard and stood, politely returning his smile, and answering him in a similar fashion. "If you could, the reading room where we were previously would be acceptable. There are a few texts I wish to revisit."

He led me back into the twisting, turning halls from the lobby until we were back in the quiet reading room where he'd first demonstrated the marvelous magical volume to find everything I'd requested previously. Once we were alone, however, we dropped our polite façade.

"Before we move on, I must know. How did things go in the temple?" His eyes were wide with excitement and curiosity, and I smiled triumphantly as I pulled the goblet out of my bag. He stumbled, practically falling into the chair behind him as he held out shaking hands.

I passed it to him and watched as he turned it over with wide eyes before eventually looking at me with disbelief written all over his face.

"It's... This is the Soul Goblet! I've only heard of it in legend." He swallowed hard. "I never expected to see it. I didn't think it was real." His voice almost as shaky as his hands, he returned to his reverent caressing of the goblet as he examined every inch of it.

"True, but you didn't think the globe was real either. And it turns out it was, and here we are. But I know nothing about this object, or why it presented itself to me."

I looked at Sel, who was sitting quietly beside the door. Although he'd stopped standing guard, he remained alert. I could tell he was listening with equal interest.

Jarid bit his lip, pulling his magical reference text out. When he opened the pages, his eyes had brightened. "Here. When I thought about the Soul Goblet, it brought up this."

He narrowed his eyes, lips moving as he silently read the passage again. "*Um*, huh. Well, how unfortunate," he stuttered.

I immediately knew what the problem was. "It's in the secret room we discovered, isn't it?"

He exhaled slowly. "Yeah. The room Luban also currently has under twenty-four-hour guard by direct order." He bit his cheek, drumming his fingers in a rapid staccato on the large reading table. I could see his dilemma.

"If you'd rather, I can go by myself." I didn't want him in any more trouble.

His words echoed my thoughts as if he'd read my mind. "No, I'm supposed to stay with you and make sure *you* don't get into any trouble. Besides," he added, pointing at the chain around my neck, "you've been granted Library access and have a key. According to what I understand about the Library, which granted is nowhere close to everything, it should give you full access. Regardless of what he's ordered, I don't think the guards can keep you out. Heck, *I* don't even have a key yet. At the rate I'm going, I probably won't ever get one."

A dry, humorless chuckle escaped him, and I couldn't help but feel responsible. Probably because I *was* responsible.

"Jarid–"

He stood, slamming the book shut. "Nope. I don't want to hear it. You did nothing wrong. You merely followed your conscience and did what the Library allowed you to do. As a Librarian apprentice, technically you get to tell me what to do, even without being a guest. Therefore, we're going back to the secret room." This time, the smile reached his eyes as he paused with his hand on the door. "Besides, it's not a secret anymore. With guards present full-time, we no longer have to make it through any trials to get there. The Library has decided the secret room is back in service."

I raised my eyebrows. "Really? Is that common?"

We were walking now, once again in the long hallways. As promised, the route was easier and more direct.

"Not really. To my knowledge, it has happened a few times. But only when the Library wishes. There's also been a few times where common rooms have disappeared or moved to another location entirely."

We carried on somewhat more briskly along the path.

I watched for any sign of ur'gel, unable to keep from flinching at normal sounds, even though it was a short, easy trip compared to the last time. When we arrived at the guarded door, I nervously displayed my key to the large men standing on either side of the stone door.

They moved aside immediately, either not recognizing me or not questioning my presence because of the key. It had been far easier than I could've dreamed, which made me worry more. I expected an interrogation. Easy made me nervous.

As we entered the room, the pedestal with the book Jarid

had defaced was again in the center of the room. My gaze slid past it to the tablet wall which lit up and made me question the accounts we'd learned of the Dark War in other records. It was quiet, and I thought perhaps it had told me everything it wished to for now. My eyes were drawn back to the round wall from where I'd taken my own contraband volumes and hope swelled as I set to work.

Surely, I'd find the answers in here somewhere

CHAPTER 2

I rubbed my eyes. They were gritty, and for a moment I couldn't figure out why. Then I realized it wasn't just my eyes. My entire body had seized. During the time I'd been reading, I had ended up slumped on the floor beside the bookshelf. I'd found several interesting texts and gotten carried away with my research.

Jarid had gravitated back toward the pedestal book, and a quick glance in Sel's direction demonstrated his high intelligence, and I thought he may be smarter than both Jarid *and* I put together—he was napping.

I stretched, allowing a yawn to escape.

This caught Jarid's attention and caused Sel to startle awake, blinking as he looked around for any threats.

I smiled and finished stretching. I couldn't believe how much time had passed. It always seemed to be like that when I got into a book. Part of me thought I should be careful here, though, because it was literally possible to become captured in a book.

"It's almost dinner bell." Jarid stepped down from the pedestal, a reluctant look on his face. "As the Library has gifted you with the key, you're entitled to join me and the other Librarians and apprentices in the dining hall."

My eyebrows shot up. "Are you sure that's a good idea? I mean, Luban and Kramson haven't been overly enthused about my presence."

He shrugged. "Good idea or not, the others won't be waiting for us to eat. With the amount of reading we anticipated you'd want to do … I gave my notebook to Will. They can contact us if needed. We rather expected you to want to stay as close to the Library as possible until you figured out what to do with the goblet."

"Huh. Well, I can't argue with your logic. In fact, it almost sounds as if you know me as well, or better, than I know myself." I gave him a wry smile.

When the two boys exchanged smirks however, my humor turned to irritation.

"Fine. I guess you'll show me the way then. If we're going to be eating here, maybe we can get more reading done this evening."

Jarid nodded, ignoring my surly tone, and we followed him to a large dining hall. Once again, the Library surprised me. Although it appeared roomy on the outside, the depth and breadth of the place astonished me, with this single chamber easily as long as the Library on the outside.

We turned the corner and he opened the right side of a large wooden set of double doors. As we entered a cavernous room, with row after row of long tables, I halted. Each table looked as though it could seat at least a hundred guests. The tables themselves were covered in a variety of foods, many of which I didn't recognize, but as we headed for an empty spot near the back, several of my favorite dishes appeared on the table in front of us.

I couldn't contain my amazement and was positive my eyebrows were so high the potential for them getting stuck in my hairline was a real threat. I knew my suspicion was correct when he gave me a knowing smile.

"Yeah, fairly sure I looked like you the first time I was allowed in here as well. Unlike Will, who has a family, I grew up in a variety of orphanages and spent some time on the streets in Sunland and bountiful foodstuffs weren't on the menu for me. I came here, and basically all my dreams had come true. There's nothing quite like a table anticipating your every food desire when you've spent half your life hungry."

I narrowed my eyes, considering his last statement while I tried to avoid him thinking I pitied him in anyway. It was heartbreaking thinking of him being a young, hungry street rat, but I kept my face as neutral as I could.

He waved a hand in denial. "Okay, not quite everything. Most things. At least those which are culturally acceptable in the areas where the Library dwells."

I cocked my head. "Where the Library dwells? Do you mean there's different foods for different parts of the Library?"

"I've never tried to ask. Let's just say depending on where the apprentice or Librarian comes from, the food on the table changes. In my case, it's been normal human fare. But some of the other people from well, let's just say more remote regions, can have more peculiar tastes."

"Interesting." My voice trailed off as I sat down at an empty spot and began to reach for the food, before stopping and looking at him again. "Do I need to wait for something, or can we help ourselves here?"

I realized with a fair amount of surprise just how accustomed I'd become to being on my own. It hadn't even occurred to me to wait for a servant or prayer, or formality of any kind. Traveling and the road had really rubbed off on me, undoing a lifetime of expectations.

"No, people come and go from here depending on their projects. Which means we generally eat on a rotating schedule. And yes, you're expected to help yourself." He sat across from me as Sel snagged a spot beside me and we all loaded our plates.

Sel was already halfway through his second helping when another apprentice approached us, his long brown robes rolled up at the elbows as he crossed his arms and planted his feet shoulder width apart. He arched one arrogant eyebrow at me and gave Jarid a condemning look.

"What are they doing here? You know better. Only Librarians and their servants are allowed in here."

Jarid closed his eyes and gave me a suffering look, almost as if he'd been expecting this, then pushed himself back from the table to stand and face the judgmental apprentice. He gestured to us, speaking mildly while maintaining a calm expression.

"She's a new Librarian, and he *is* her servant. I've already cleared everything with Kramson. Not that it's any of your business." His tone remained neutral the entire time, but I winced the moment he added the 'none of your business' part. In my experience, those words were generally followed by trouble.

Something about the way the other apprentice looked at me, his gaze hardening when he'd spotted my ears, also led me to believe he was a human who detested elves as much as many elves detested humans. Rolling my eyes, I prepared for a showdown with a narrow-minded bigot.

"I don't care who you talked to. I have seniority, and I'm telling you they don't belong here. If you know what's best for you, you'll take them, scram, and not bother coming back."

Jarid exhaled slowly and I could practically see him counting to ten as he faced the other apprentice. Although shorter by a few inches, the other boy was broader in the shoulders. I couldn't help but fear for his safety.

I stood quickly and came around to his side. Sel continued to eat, but he watched the situation intently as he chewed. I knew if anything happened to me, he would do his best to protect me. Which meant I needed to diffuse the situation immediately, before anyone got injured.

Before I could speak, Jarid crossed his arms and leaned into the other man's space. "Franse, you know, as well as I do, you've got no authority or seniority over me. What exactly do you think you're going to do in front of everyone?"

Franse narrowed his eyes, practically sneering now. "Well, I've never liked you, so why don't I start by making sure your nose doesn't go back to the same ugly shape when I've finished rearranging it? I'll see what I'm in the mood for once *that* task is complete."

I looked around at the other tables, noticing we were fast becoming the center of interested gazes, the same way we had when the slaver eyed up Gwen and her wolves.

I sighed, stepping in front of Jarid and held my hand out for Franse to shake. When he didn't accept, I dropped it and spoke blithely, as if nothing was amiss.

"I'm sorry, we haven't been properly introduced. My name is Rhin. I'm visiting from Cliffside. The Library has seen fit to give me a key of my own to facilitate my research. From what I understand, a key means I'm allowed within this facility. Your friend had been assigned to me previously by the head Librarian, Luban, and again today by Kramson. If you have any concerns with this, you are welcome to bring them up with either of those gentlemen."

His face went positively purple as his eyes bulged out. I watched a vein in the right side of his temple begin to pulse. It was easy to see he was inappropriately angry given my polite tone and matter-of-fact statements.

As someone used to dealing with diplomacy in the elf world, I was surprised at the intensity of his reaction to my little speech. Obviously, the bad blood between them went deeper than I understood. Which meant, of course, it was unlikely he would leave us alone.

His next words exploded in a shriek, almost tumbling over

each other in the speed they were uttered. "How dare you speak to me? A dirty elf. I can't even believe they let your filthy kind into a place like this."

His rant took off from there, but the moment he began name calling I tuned him out. It was obvious I wasn't dealing with an entirely sane man, so I considered my next move. If he couldn't be reasoned with, we needed to be ready to act. I began listening again in time to hear him casting aspersions on not only my parents, but my entire lineage.

I held up a hand, stopping him dead. "All right. It appears to me I am speaking to either an idiot or a madman. I do not know you well enough to decide which, but it's clear you aren't worth my time."

As Franse filled up with air and fury, I took the biggest chance I'd yet taken. "Library? Can you do something about him? This apprentice does not seem to value the sanctity of your space as he should."

I wasn't sure if anything would happen, but I was curious. If the Library listened to people when they spoke to it, perhaps if I asked it directly to help me something might happen. Otherwise, I would be the one looking like an idiot, not him. I only hoped if the Library didn't answer my unconscious fighting skills were still hanging around to help me out.

A small crowd had formed around the three of us by now.

Sel remained seated, but he'd placed his fork down while he watched attentively. He seemed ready to leap over the table at a moment's notice.

Jarid's hands were tight fists and he rocked slightly back and forth on the balls of his feet.

Franse still looked as if his head would explode.

In fact, his face was so purple I was worried he'd explode from pressure. I blinked, and the next moment his fist was flying toward my face. I ducked, blocking with my hand.

When I opened my eyes, he was kneeling on the floor at my

feet, whimpering as I gripped his fist in my left hand. I let go, stunned as he shuddered and wept holding his crushed hand.

As my wits returned, I quickly pretended I'd known what would happen all along. "I think we have proof. The Library has spoken."

I spoke in a voice loud enough to carry, trying to fill it with the same grandeur I'd heard my father use for announcements. "I will be passing details of this altercation along to the head Librarian now. Perhaps you can reconsider your animosity toward others who aren't the same as you."

When I recalled Luban's reaction to the wolves and Loglan, I knew it was unlikely for Franse to experience an awakening about the wisdom of judging people as a group. At least he left quickly, shooting scared glances back at me as he stumbled past benches to the door.

I turned to the guys, my heart racing. "Well, gentlemen, I believe I've had enough to eat. Perhaps it's time for us to retire and discuss other items?"

I widened and relaxed my eyes, and both nodded.

We walked to the door without delay or speaking. Once we were within the safety of the reading room, we waited until the door was shut, then began to chuckle.

"What was that?" The awe in Jarid's voice was audible.

I shrugged, holding both hands up in front of my face.

"I have no idea. I asked the Library for help, anticipating maybe someone would come by. When he threw that punch, I closed my eyes. I have absolutely no idea how my hand caught his and was able to squeeze hard enough to bring him to his knees." I grimaced. "I'm a Librarian, a scholar, not a strong woman. It must have been the Library answering me, or maybe something left over from reading the tablets about Beru."

He whistled appreciatively. "Well, whatever it was, Franse will think twice about bothering you again." He rolled his eyes, adding, "Me, on the other hand? I'm sure I'll be fair game the moment your back is turned."

I looked at him with an instant pit of dread in my stomach. I knew he was right. "The Library isn't as safe as I thought. I'm beginning to think carrying the goblet in my bag, on my person constantly, isn't the best place for it. I need to find a hiding spot, at least until I can figure out what it does or discover what my next move should be.

"I know of one way you might be able to conceal it," He spoke slowly as he thought his idea through. "In the room where we found the other books on Onen Suun, there was a way to put something into a text. To hide objects inside a book."

A bark of laughter escaped me. "It's funny you should mention that. I was thinking before we went to eat how my penchant for getting lost in a book could be a real risk instead of merely a figure of speech."

He bobbed his head in agreement. "It's crossed my mind a few times over the years as well. Some of the things I've seen in the last five years have been rather strange."

All humor faded as I looked at him, feeling an urgency I hadn't before supper. "Let's go back to the room now. Show me what you're talking about and I can decide after. All I know for certain is there are people we can't trust here, and I'm not willing to let the goblet fall into the wrong hands."

CHAPTER 3

We headed back to the place I'd begun to think of as my personal secret chamber. Jarid was motivated in a way I'd never seen before, his eyes bright and head held high. I wasn't sure if it was the altercation with Franse which had brought the spring to his step, or the thought of using a text he'd always been fascinated by.

Either way, when we returned to the Suun Room the guards again stepped aside unquestioningly when I flashed my key. Once inside, he pulled out his wonderful reference volume, flipped the page, concentrated, then closed it with an ear-to-ear grin.

"So, interesting thing here. It says the book we need for this is one of the books in your bag. The one neither of us could read."

A wave of surprise filled me, followed immediately by amusement. The Library had foreseen my needs and given me the exact tools I required before I knew I needed them. I was rapidly discovering I simply needed to ask the correct questions, which still slowed me down. I couldn't blame the Library for that though as it was more my issue than anything else. I shook my head as I looked at the walls around me. Not for the first time I had a sense the Library was able to hear my thoughts. Or maybe it was simply omniscient.

"Figures. I knew there was a reason I wanted that book. I'd thought about dropping it off somewhere, but the weird little voice I've been hearing in my head told me I'd need it soon. Now, I'm starting to wonder if that little voice isn't my conscience after all."

I looked around dramatically, squinting and shifting my eyes from side to side while both the guys chuckled. It was funny, but at the same time, I meant it. Things seemed to be happening for a reason, whether we understood why or not.

I pulled the richly bound volume out of my bag, glancing at the plain cover for a moment. "I think the reason neither of us could read this is because it's not words yet." My words were halting as I looked at the book, thinking as I spoke.

"I'm not sure. I mean, I knew of this particular book's existence, but I had no idea it was one of the books you had in your bag until now. I just assumed it was a book written in a language I couldn't read."

I raised my eyebrows in disbelief.

He flinched from my glare and whined, "What? I'm not a full Librarian yet, I only know about twenty or so languages, and most of those are only to read, not speak. There's probably another hundred or more I don't know, and who knows how many other languages we aren't even aware of."

I reluctantly allowed him his explanation and passed the book over so he could examine it. When his face lit up, I was certain it was the right book.

"So, you said we can use this book to keep the goblet safe? How?"

He sat down on a square of the floor, crossing his legs as he opened the book between them and looked back at me. "As I understand it, this book will allow you to store objects within it. There is a spell, but it's easy. It uses magic already bound within the pages of the book itself from nature, so the person casting it doesn't need to have their own magic. Once the item is inside, you can devise a series of tests or puzzles to keep the item safe. To retrieve the object, the person has to solve them to get to the page where the object will be waiting for them."

My eyes widened. "You mean, tests like the way the Library tested me to get to this room?"

"Exactly." He looked around, a mixture of fondness, irritation, and approval on his face as he surveyed the walls around us. "The Library is very particular. I've heard rumors it's alive, but others say it's a collection of beings we can understand if they choose to speak to us. Either way, the Library is a sentient being. Many of the objects within it seem to retain or possess the same qualities."

He pointed at the key around my neck.

"I haven't been lucky enough to attain one yet, but I believe once a Librarian is gifted with a key, it will help direct any natural magic they possess, as well as give other abilities when the Library sees fit."

I rested my hand on my shirt, feeling the pulse of the key beneath it, comforting against my skin. The idea I could end up with powers beyond what the Library had already bestowed upon me was both frightening and exciting. I hoped I'd be able to cope with what the Library threw at me, and it wasn't wrong in its assessment of my abilities.

"How does the book work?"

He held up the same finger he'd used to point at my key, then flipped through his own book. He stopped, looked at the shelf directly behind us and pulled a smaller, cream-colored volume off the shelf. "The spell should be in here. As well as instructions on how to craft your puzzle, or puzzles, to protect it.

Greedily, I accepted the book and settled in to read. Although it had less than fifty pages, I read and reread several of the entries until I was certain I had them firmly locked inside my memory. While not the most powerful elf in my family magically, I'd always felt as if my ability to retain information and details was more natural to me than others, either through extensive practice or innate ability.

When I looked up, it was to find both boys watching me.

Jarid was tapping his fingers impatiently against his leg while Sel was trying to keep his face flat and emotionless, but he was leaning so far over I could almost feel his breath on my neck. When I caught him, he blushed and moved back, pretending he hadn't been trying to read over my shoulder.

I smirked before standing and stretching my stiff muscles, then took the cream-colored book, along with the red volume, over to the pedestal. At some point between when we'd left the Suun Room and returned from supper, the volume which had been there had vanished, leaving an empty workspace, as if the Library expected us to need a place to put other books.

I glanced at the room, putting that idea behind me when nothing but the expected silence from the walls greeted me. The words were written in old Elvish, which I spoke fluently. I traced the words with my fingers as I read aloud.

A slight shifting of the items within my satchel startled me, and I realized the goblet was still inside. Without breaking my concentration, I flipped the leather bag open and withdrew the goblet, placing it on top of the book, in the center just above the spine. As I recited the words, the key on my chest became almost uncomfortably warm.

Something was happening involving the Library's magic.

It was working!

The words weren't complicated. In fact, it seemed like a prayer to the God of Learning and Knowledge, specifically to keep the information within the book safe. As I spoke, midway through the first page, the goblet began to glow. I stuttered as the edges of the metal became vague and cloudy but pushed on. Before I knew it, it seemed to melt.

It poured into the red bound book as I tried to speak the

incantation through a strange tightness in my chest. I pushed through my astonishment until there was no sight of the goblet.

I finished the last paragraph and paused to let the events sink in. The goblet was gone, as were the words from the red text. I closed the cream-colored book I'd used for the spell, turning to the guys, who waited at the bottom of the podium with bright, curious eyes.

"Now what?" I tilted my head as I waited for an answer.

Jarid looked at me blankly for a moment, pursing his lips before finally responding with a hint of confused irritation present in his voice. "I'm not sure. I mean, you're the one who read the instruction manual. What did it say?"

I rolled my eyes, but realized he was right. They'd merely watched from the sidelines while I figured out the spell and performed it. I laid out what I had read for him.

"It basically showed me I needed to create a test so I would be able to get back to the goblet, but only I or someone I thought worthy..." I winced, only now understanding the implications of what I'd read. "I guess it's a failsafe, in case I die or don't make it back to the book."

He nodded solemnly. "In that case, it should be a test specific to you and things only you or someone close to you would know. Or if you're worried it will be a thousand years until someone finds it, you might want to ensure someone who doesn't know anything about you can solve it." He looked at the book. "There is a chance the goblet truly could be lost forever if no one can solve your puzzles."

"Yeah, good point, but not one I'm comfortable thinking about." I gnawed on my lower lip, trying to decide which was the better option. Something specific to me, or something an individual who didn't know me, but who I'd be happy with having the goblet, would be able to retrieve it.

I wrinkled my nose as I looked at him. "Maybe a combination of the two?"

He nodded. "Sure. What were you thinking?"

I stared at the book, seeing Sel out of the corner of my eyes watching with an attentive expression and stopped. "Well here's the thing. I hadn't really. Maybe some riddles?"

"To test a person's intelligence. Or learning? There are plenty of riddles anyone who's had any kind of education would get, and others which could be more of a puzzle."

"Good point." Absently biting at my thumbnail, I racked my brain for specifics. "Well, there's one riddle coming to mind, but it might be too easy."

When they waited for me to tell them, I reluctantly elaborated. "I learned this one almost as soon as I learned to read. What travels on four legs in the morning, two legs in the afternoon, and three legs in the evening?"

They furrowed their eyebrows, looking first at each other, then back at me blankly. I felt a little more confident and less silly now I knew neither had heard it before.

"Man. Well, humans anyway."

At the same instant, their faces brightened with comprehension.

"I get it!" Sel smiled. "Babies crawl, adults walk upright, and the elderly sometimes walk with a cane."

"It may not be the most difficult, but it should ensure someone had basic education, at least in the art of reasoning. Do you want to use it?" Jarid paused, adding, "Of course, we both know the answer now and we would be able to access the goblet as well."

I nodded, having already considered that. "Honestly, after what we've been through together, in addition to Will and Gwen, I can't think of anyone else I'd trust more to use this goblet for the right reasons. So, I fully expect either of you to be able to access the goblet if I..."

I let my sentence trail off. I could see they understood, and I didn't need to finish my fatalistic line of thinking. I moved on briskly. "So, the first one is done."

I looked down at the cream-colored book, flipping through

the pages as I considered the best way to activate the riddle as a test. It appeared to be relatively straightforward. There was another short paragraph to say, and the riddle should go into the book, the same way the goblet had.

Once finished, I nodded with satisfaction.

"There, I can read it, can you?" I turned the page for him to see, the bindings soft beneath my hand.

He squinted, smiling sheepishly as he answered. "Not well, but I can see it's there. My Elvish isn't what it should be for a Librarian. I've been studying hard, don't worry," he added quickly.

I looked at Sel, but he shook his head. He didn't know how to read Elvish. Obviously, that would limit anyone who could find the goblet to someone who could speak and read Elvish. An unintended puzzle all by itself, I realized with surprise. It hadn't been intentional but would serve well as a second test.

As I watched, the pages in the book changed, adjusting to the content. At the back of the book, the pages were filling with scrawling script, along with page after page of images of the goblet, which when placed together approximately formed the size. I'd never seen this kind of magic before, and it was fascinating to watch.

"We should have at least two more tasks," Sel piped up.

I tilted my head to the side, surprised he had an opinion on it. "How come?"

His lip quirked up in a half-smile. "Because every good quest should have at least three tasks to accomplish. What about one based on character?"

I narrowed my eyes as I considered his idea. "Interesting. Like what? How would I create a test specifically for character?"

Sel looked at the book. "I'm not entirely sure. Maybe give them a choice? Between the goblet, which they may or may not be looking for specifically, and something most beings would desire more?"

I hummed as I thought it through. Something everyone would desire, regardless of who they were. My eyes widened as I looked at them. "What does almost everyone on this planet find valuable?"

They answered in unison.

"Fortune," Sel pronounced, adding an emphatic nod.

"Freedom." Jarid corrected, wrinkling his forehead as he considered Sel.

I looked between them, surprised. I would've thought they would have answered the other way around, given one had been a slave technically his whole life and the other had no need for money, since his needs were provided for by the Library. Perhaps I was showing my own biases again.

"Okay, freedom and fortune. How about both? Offering the reader enough to live on for the rest of their lives wherever they choose or the prize at the end of the book instead?"

Jarid grimaced. "Unless they're actually searching for the goblet, and even if they are, I think most people would pick freedom and fortune over a vague prize at the end of the book."

Sel enthusiastically agreed. "It's perfect. So how are you going to do it?"

I could feel a devilish smile creep over my face.

"Well..." I paused dramatically to draw out the tension. "I'll just ask them, 'Would they rather?'"

Jarid leaned back, eyebrows raised as he considered it. "You mean, ask them if they had a choice between solving the puzzle and getting to the end, or living free of ownership and financial worries, which they would choose?"

"Why not? Sometimes the hardest tasks have the easiest answers." I liked the simplicity. A question with a yes or no was simple yet telling. If riches could distract someone, they weren't the right person to have the goblet. I smiled and turned back to the book, repeating another short paragraph, and watched as the words went across the page and demanded the reader choose.

It was clever the way the book rearranged itself. Whoever was reading had to choose one of two phrases. Depending on which they spoke, they would either be closer to the goblet, or the words themselves would vanish from the page and leave the reader with nothing.

I felt marginally guilty. I was, in a sense, lying to the unknown reader about their options. Hopefully, it would be myself or one of my friends in the worst-case scenario, and they should know the correct answer and not be led astray. My conscience slightly lessened, I smiled at the guys.

"There, part two is over. Now, one more."

CHAPTER 4

Once the goblet was protected, we had to figure out what the Library wanted us to find next. I thought back to the texts in my family's library, and the artifacts it had mentioned. But those accounts had been vague. I hadn't even known the goblet was one of the artifacts until I'd found it, which didn't give me much to go on.

All I knew for certain was the goblet was safe, tucked into a book in my satchel close to my body. Although it was still on me, unless you knew what you were looking for and where, it was as safe as it could be under any lock and key. If only information about the other artifacts was easier to find.

By now it was getting late and my eyes were telling me they didn't have long before they would become heavy and any further quest for knowledge would become futile. I began to pack up my books, pausing when I heard an excited exclamation from the other side of the room.

Jarid had returned to the pedestal, and I wasn't sure when or how, but the book he'd been looking at the first time we came into the room had reappeared. He was pointing at something within its pages.

It made things worse.

Jarid apologized. "I know. It sucks. But it makes sense, doesn't it? First you found the Soul Goblet, now we need to find the Heart Stone."

Sel had crept close enough to peer at the page and looked at me. "We should tell the others."

"We will, but let's wait until morning," Jarid agreed. "I think we all could use some rest. After all, we'll need to find someone who can get us there. And it's not a journey to even think of beginning at night."

WE RESET the traps on the room as best we could before leaving. My new sense of being unable to trust everyone within the Library demanded I protect the items within. The Library was fully capable of keeping out those it didn't wish to see, but I felt the need to do something on top of what I hoped it would do to keep the room safe.

As we left the room, I paused long enough to see if the guards were able to open the door. One had merely rolled his eyes, but the other had tried and failed. A look of stunned bewilderment was immediately followed by uneasiness, and the guards had looked at each other with wide eyes as we waved and left without waiting for them to recover from the surprise. I was confident it would hold, even if I did feel a little bad for them.

Jarid smirked as we walked away. Once we were out of earshot he spoke in a low voice, "Kramson isn't going to be happy."

I knew he was right, but I couldn't chance leaving the room open just to keep the Librarian happy, so I just shrugged. Wordlessly, I followed him to the rooms he'd procured.

The lodgings for the night were in the wing with the other plain Librarian single bedrooms. The building reminded me a little of priests, in the way they lived a simple life, with the bare minimum of necessities. A fleeting thought about how much this would've bothered me a month ago crossed my mind, but this new incarnation of myself was merely grateful for a clean, relatively soft space to lay my head. Compared to the forest floor, the bed was positively luxurious.

I could tell Sel was uncomfortable leaving me alone, but our rooms were beside each other and clearly meant for only one Librarian or apprentice at a time, so he had no choice. Once he ensured I was safely in my room, I was left with only my thoughts for company.

And such thoughts they were. With everything which had happened running through my head, my eyelids felt like they'd never close, even though they were so heavy I couldn't keep them open if I tried.

After what felt like mere moments, I opened them again, feeling frustrated and tired. I couldn't stop replaying my trip from the Low Forest to Abrecem Secer. To my surprise, the faint light of dawn was creeping through my room. Apparently, I'd slept through the entire night.

I quickly freshened up with the bowl of water in the corner, shivering from the chilly temperatures. I hadn't had to break through a layer of ice, but it felt nearly as cold. I debated going back to bed to warm up but dressed instead.

Once warmer, I checked my satchel to make sure I had all the books as well as my lonely change of clothes. The ones I was wearing now weren't too dirty, but I needed to either have a true bath or buy something new as I was beginning to feel unpleasantly ripe.

I tiptoed into the hallway, knocking softly on the door beside mine. A muffled yelp followed by a thump made me wince. It sounded like Sel had fallen out of bed. My suspicions were confirmed when he opened the door, bleary-eyed and briskly rubbing his backside.

"Sorry. I must've overslept. Give me a moment and I'll be ready. Jarid's in the room beside me."

I gave him what I hoped was a sympathetic smile before moving on to see if Jarid was awake. He must've heard the commotion, because a split second before I knocked, he opened his door, appearing fresh and ready to go.

"Ready to travel?" He closed the door and tilted his head, waiting for me to reply.

Hesitancy gripped me. "Ready, and not ready," I admitted. "You know I'd rather stay here. The Library has so many mysteries to explore."

He nodded; his eyes warm. "Yeah, I understand. I don't get nearly the time nor opportunity to discover everything I'd like to know about, either. As an apprentice, there's always more work to do for someone else. But you're a Librarian, so you have far fewer constraints."

He bit his lip, and I watched as a shadow of doubt flashed across his face.

"What is it?" A sinking feeling in my stomach warned me leaving wasn't going to be as simple as I hoped.

"Well, the thing is, I know you're a Librarian and all, because the Library wanted you to have a key, but all the Librarians I know are pretty much tied to the Library. I can't remember the last time one of them went anywhere or explored anything."

"I see. Well, the Library did give me a key. Even before I got the key I was on a quest, so it must be okay with me traveling away from here." I stopped, looking around the narrow hallway. Part of me expected the Library to answer, but I was greeted by silence.

I wasn't sure when I'd gotten into the habit of thinking of the Library as a living, breathing entity, but I did. I felt she was wise and all-knowing, and somehow, she was another friend I was bringing with me, wherever I went. But I couldn't tell the guys. They'd think I was crazy.

"Ready," Sel appeared, looking slightly out of breath as he shut the door behind him.

We followed Jarid down the hall, and were almost to the entrance when Kramson appeared, his face flushed, and eyebrows knitted together so they almost appeared to be a single unit.

"Where do you think you're going? Librarians need to stay within the Library. The only reason you could leave the last time is because I gave the key to you after you'd already left."

Although I knew what Kramson was referring to, I was still irritated at the idea anyone would tell me what I could do. A pit in my stomach hardened when I realized he was also looking at Jarid.

"I'm sorry you feel that way. But the Library already knows where I'm going, since it gave me the information necessary to get there. In my mind, this means the Library has decided she's okay with this happening."

His eyes narrowed further, now hardly slits in his round face. "It may be the case, assuming you are correct. And if so, I may not be able to stop *you*. Jarid, however, must remain. Even if you are acting on the Library's wishes, he's an apprentice only, and not entitled to the same freedoms and luxuries as a full Librarian."

I opened my mouth to argue, but he placed a hand on my sleeve and shook his head.

"It's okay. He's right. I had a feeling me leaving would be a problem, and I'm content to stay behind. You still have your book, right?"

At the mention of books, Kramson turned his glare back to me.

"I insist you tell me which books you're taking with you. In fact, books are not allowed to leave the premises without express permission from the Head Librarian."

I raised an eyebrow, giving him a cool look. "The Library knows which books I'm taking. That's good enough. They'll come back when I come back. But I need to leave, and I need to bring them with me."

I watched as he worked to regain control of his obviously increasing frustration. He took several deep breaths, closed his eyes, and exhaled slowly before opening them and pressing his lips together tightly.

"Fine. You can leave and take the books you currently have in your possession. But Jarid needs to stay, and you need to take those protections down from the Library. We haven't started cataloging the books yet. Since you left the Suun Room last night, the guards haven't been able to get in, and when I tried, neither could I. Unacceptable." He crossed his arms as he waited for my answer.

"Look, Kramson. I can't trust everyone in the Library is doing what's best for this place, let alone all Lynia. That's the reason we reset the traps in the first place. But if the Library wants you in there, she'll let you in. After all, she let me in."

Raising an eyebrow, I waited for him to argue.

He sputtered, and even stomped his feet once, but didn't argue further.

We looked at each other for a moment as he regained his control, and I saw recognition and something else I didn't recognize pass over his face.

Kramson nodded, letting another sigh escape. "If you are not going to remove your protections, I expect you to return as soon as possible. It appears the Library has decided you will be the Librarian who must catalogue that room."

"Thank you. I'll return as soon as I can. But first, the Library would like me to find something not within its holdings." I looked at Jarid, disappointment coloring my words. "I wish you could come, but I understand. I'll keep in touch the same as before."

He gave me a weak smile. "I wish I could, too. Fu Shen be with you. I'll keep looking for any clues here that may be of use while you're away."

I clasped his hand briefly and was about to walk away before I remembered Will had my copy of the two-way book.

Instead, I leaned in as if I was going to hug him. His eyes widened as I slipped the book into his hands and he nodded almost imperceptibly as he shifted, hiding the book from Kramson's view. I stepped back with a smile, then turned and walked out of the Library.

I caught Sel's nervous glance back at the imposing building before it disappeared behind us as we headed to the edge of town to find Gwen and her wolves.

CHAPTER 5

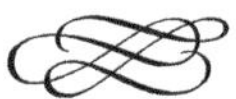

I had no idea where we were supposed to meet, only a vague idea it was somewhere on the outskirts of the city. Will had taken her somewhere supposedly safe to set up camp. Part of me hoped he was there too, but another part hoped he wasn't. I pushed the conflicting emotions aside, telling myself I wanted my friends safe and together. I decided it was simply because he could be so irritating, I was torn about his presence with her at the campsite.

I remembered the way we'd entered the city and started retracing our route to the outskirts from there. If there was one thing I was good for, it was remembering details. I may not be the best on a trail, even if I had come a long way during our journey, but I could certainly guide us back the way we'd come. The only question was whether we'd find our friends along the same route.

We wound our way through the streets until we reached the edge of town. We paused briefly, sharing a silent moment as we looked at the beautiful skyline behind us, so different from Sunglen but equally impressive with its dark, sparkly spires instead of the golden glass I'd been awed by.

Although Starside wasn't the magical kingdom of sweetness and light the naïve, untraveled, younger me had imagined it would be, the city, and particularly the Library, had quickly become a place I felt like I belonged. But time was wasting, and we had another long journey ahead of us.

"Ready?" I raised an eyebrow at my only companion.

His eyes practically sparkled. "Absolutely milady ... I mean, Rhin. Any ideas where we should look for her?"

I shook my head, wrinkling my nose. "Not really, although knowing her and the wolves, I expect they'd prefer a quiet area with a bit of shade. Hidden. Out of the way."

"I'm sure they didn't go far, did they?"

I shrugged, uneasy with my lack of answers when it came to finding my friend.

We'd been walking as we spoke and were finally nearing the edge of the city.

I wasn't entirely sure where she would be, but knew it had to be somewhere nearby. After all, she wouldn't leave without me. It felt odd to be backtracking when I needed to go the other direction, but I wasn't comfortable going anywhere without Gwen at my side. And it might be nice to have Will there for support as well, although I was less enthused about him.

"What's a princess like you doing in a place like this?"

I turned around, my pulse quickening at the sound of a loud, raspy male voice calling out to us. For a split second, I was bewildered and a little afraid. Was it another slaver? But even before I turned my brain caught up and I recognized the voice.

Will was leaning on a turned over carriage as if he'd been waiting the whole time for us to show up. He waved. "Yup, it's me."

"Well, speaking of things which can be described as irritating." I smiled and raised an eyebrow, waiting for his comeback as he ambled toward me.

His arms swung lazily at his sides, seemingly content to

move slow and in no apparent dismay at being described as irritating.

"I figured I'd keep a lookout for you." He yawned, covering his mouth.

Now I really was curious how long he'd been waiting there for us.

He dressed the same as the first time I saw him but looked refreshed despite the yawn. Even so, I had the sneaking suspicion he'd been there all night. Looking back at the street we'd just passed through it was a miracle he'd managed to stay in one piece if that was the case. It fit the bill perfectly as a dark alley where you could potentially get attacked in broad daylight, let alone at night.

"Thanks. We know where we need to look for the next thing, but I need to find Gwen first. Can you take us to her?"

He chuckled. "Sure can. But your friend has some pretty strange ideas about what makes a good place to camp." He shook his head, an amused expression on his face. "It wasn't my choice of venues for an overnight camping spot, so I decided to come and wait around here for you. It was a little too removed from civilization for my liking. But don't worry, we'll be there in no time."

My spirits sank, but I should have expected this. I wasn't thrilled about having to travel before we could travel, but it was just like her to want to be away from everyone. "We should get moving. Our trip isn't going to be particularly easy or short."

His eyes became intent, curiosity replacing the normally irritating smugness.

"We're going to have to get to the Northwestern Lands somehow. The next item I need to find is something known as the Heart Stone"

I'd dropped my voice, so it was a surprise when he shushed me.

His eyes darted everywhere as if worried we'd be overheard by unfriendly ears. He relaxed at the sight of the empty alley but kept a finger to his lips for a beat longer anyway. "We'll talk more along the way. But not here. I'll take you to find your friend."

I quickly discovered when he'd mentioned her choice of campsite wasn't particularly comfortable, he'd been understating the facts. Not only was it not a comfortable trip there, the actual campsite was right on the edge of a mountain. The weather had been ideal for traveling so far, but as the wind cut through my tunic the higher we climbed, I wholeheartedly agreed with his assessment.

"She's even crazier than I thought," I muttered under my breath, earning a smirk from Will. I glared back.

We both knew I was irritated he was right, not just because of the unpleasant weather.

"Almost there." His words were barely audible and stolen by the wind almost before I could hear them.

Luckily, he hadn't been exaggerating. Just around the next curve of the mountain I saw a small enclosure. It was warmer here, although still not ideal for a comfortable visit. We wouldn't be staying long. I hoped.

A large white wolf bounded out from behind a tree and I gasped before I was able to stop myself. As soon as I recognized Swift, his tongue lolling good-naturedly out of his mouth, a smile split my face.

"Swift! I've missed you."

It felt silly talking to the wolf until he came over to nuzzle my hand. When I gingerly placed it on his head, he allowed me to pat him.

He watched me with wide, intelligent eyes for a moment before turning to walk a few paces. He paused, turned, and repeated the movement. I looked at the guys, then followed with a feeling Swift knew exactly what he was doing.

For a moment it looked like he was leading us into the side of the mountain itself, but as I got closer, I saw a small crack between the mountain and a large pine tree. Barely big enough for an adult male to walk through, it was completely obscured from the view of anyone who didn't already know it was there. When I emerged on the other side, it was to the welcome sight of Gwen, calmly preparing a meal beside the fire.

I arched a brow and turned to Will. "Did you know she was back here?"

He shook his head, looking around in as much disbelief as I felt. "No, when I left her to build her camp last night, she'd implied the thicket of trees we walked through would suit them fine, but I had no idea this was behind it."

I nodded, his wide-eyed look supporting his statement. Somehow, she'd managed to find an alcove completely hidden from the elements. Although the ceiling was open to air, making it suitable for a fire, it was enclosed by rocks on three sides and hidden by the trees on the other. At one point there must've been a landslide or cave-in, but now it made a perfect camp site.

At the sound of our muffled conversation, she turned, leaping from her seat to launch herself at me.

My arms reflexively went out, enjoying the spontaneous and joyful hug bestowed upon me. A moment earlier I'd been frozen by the winds. Now I was warm and happy.

She pulled back, her soft eyes sparkling with pleasure as she first smiled at me, then included the guys with a small nod of her head.

"It's wonderful to see you. It's funny, because I'm used to spending my time alone with the wolves, but I *may* have missed you. Strange really. Maybe I've gotten used to being around others. It was quiet last night, and a little lonely." The corner of her lip quirked up in a bashful smile.

My heart swelled at her admission. I'd been worried about her when I fell asleep last night *and* when I'd awoken this morning. I was surprised how much I'd thought about her, considering how well I'd managed to push away my concern about my family.

"It was weird being away from you, too." My words were soft, but even as I spoke, I knew there was more I could share.

"What did you find out?" She moved back to the fire and picked up a small animal she'd been skinning, glancing up at me. She kept her eyes focused on the animal for the most part, but when I didn't answer right away, she looked up again.

I sat down beside her, watching as her graceful hands made short work of it.

"We discovered something about the Heart Stone. It sounds like it's related to the Soul Goblet I found on Bomrega Island. I think it's part of a ritual alluded to in the books I read earlier at Cliffside. If we can find it, I think we may be able to perform the ritual correctly this time, the one Suun had initially planned before he changed to the one he used to imprison Dag'draath."

"Fantastic! So, where do we go next?"

I loved the way she didn't question my theory, trusting I knew what I was talking about. It made me feel proud, somehow, knowing she thought I was every bit as capable as her in my own way.

"See, here's where it gets a little trickier." I was reluctant to break the mood of excitement but wanted her to have all the facts before she agreed to come. "Jarid believes it's hidden in the Northwestern Lands. We need to find a way back through the Low Forest to get there and find its hiding place."

Her face fell. "Well, I was hoping it was closer, but that's not so bad." She turned to Will. "Can we ask Captain Baeley to fly us there?"

He grimaced. "Depends on a few things. The first being whether she has time, and secondly, whether her ship can go there. I don't know much about how they work, except the bit about magic, but I overheard her once when she was talking to one of the deckhands saying something about how there were places she couldn't fly because the magic didn't work."

"Really? Odd. You'd think if something was magic it would always be magic." Gwen let out an interested hum as she worked, arranging it neatly on a small rack of tree branches she'd prepared and placing it over the fire, rotisserie style.

He shrugged, watching her movements. "I don't know. But if you want to ask her, we can head back into the city and see if she's at the docks. We can only try, right?"

I stared at the naked remains of the small creature, watching her give it a quarter turn. "Hopefully, you heard wrong about the magic."

ONCE OUR BELLIES were full of the small animal, I helped her repack her gear and we headed back down the mountain into Starside. I was hopeful Captain Baeley would be able to help us, because otherwise, the distance we needed to travel was far, and innumerable potential obstacles stood in our way. We'd already been attacked by ur'gel in the Low Forest, and creator only knew what awaited us between here and the North-western Lands. I also hoped the money I'd given Will would be enough. Even with what I'd taken from Cliffside before I'd left, we were running lower on funds than I'd like, and so far, the Library hadn't seen fit to provide any practical resources.

IT WAS midday when we arrived at the docks, and they were as busy as they'd been when we first met the captain. For a moment, I worried her ship was gone. An airship to my right departed, gently pushing away like a boat drifting on the water, and exposed the proud, familiar vessel behind it.

She stood on the dock supervising the reloading and didn't immediately notice our small group. When she did, she turned and gave a cheery wave. "Ahoy there! Does this mean you'll be wanting to get back to Sunglen now?"

Will looked at us, and when I gestured at him to speak, he turned to her and told her our intentions. "So, Rhin says she needs to get to the Northwestern Lands."

I waited, breath caught in my chest as her eyes widened and narrowed. I knew instantly I wasn't going to like her answer.

CHAPTER 6

"Have you been smoking Jimsonweed? Are you high right now?" She was practically bellowing at us. It was easy to guess she wasn't pleased with the question as her eyes bulged with disbelief.

I couldn't help flinching at the intensity of her reaction, not expecting the combination of confusion and anger from the otherwise stalwart captain.

Will looked at me as if to say, "I told you so," before turning to reply in a calm, soothing voice. "I know, it's not somewhere you'd normally fly. But is there a reason why you can't? Such as the danger of the journey, or something else?"

He tilted his head and I waited nervously as she worked to compose herself.

"Danger isn't something I worry about," she scoffed, bristling at the implied insult. "Have you ever seen an airship over the Low Forest? Have you?"

I'd never thought about it before, but now she mentioned it, I realized I never had. Not like that meant much, as the first time I'd ever seen an airship up close was when Will had introduced me to her.

"Look, Rhin come here!" He turned to me, his face lit with excitement and pride.

I approached, noticing Sel inching closer on his other side. I was as curious as he appeared to be, but reserved judgment. Until I saw what he'd found, it was difficult for me to get too hopeful. I was tired after the long night until I looked at the words on the page. A delighted smile spread over my face and like that, my energy was restored by a new eagerness.

"I think you've done it! This could be exactly what we need to find next."

He gave me a smug look, blinking as my words sunk in. "Could be? We both know it is. Unless you found anything more likely?"

I shook my head, not taking my eyes off the page in front of me.

"No, with the way the Library works, I'm almost certain you're on the right track," I tried to downplay my excitement, still not quite able to believe we'd reached the right conclusion. But as I read the descriptions, hope rose despite my doubts.

"The Heart Stone?" I turned, tilting my head. I'd never heard of it before.

He nodded, elaborating his answer with wild gesticulations of his hands.

"This is way more famous than even the goblet. The only problem is it's supposed to be lost in the desert of the Northwestern Territory."

My heart sank. The desert lands were notoriously difficult to cross. I'd learned about them from my tutor when I'd been younger. They were supposed to be inhabited by nothing intelligent, but the creatures who did live there were dangerous. Not to mention the weather was a formidable opponent all by itself.

"The Northwestern Territory," I was hoping if I said it out loud it wouldn't seem so bad.

Nope.

"No, I haven't." I readied myself for a biting comeback but received a satisfied smile from the fierce woman instead.

"No, you haven't. And I'll tell you why. Airships can't go over the Low Forest. We don't know why, there's no reason. They plain can't do it. Every airship crew knows this. We can go over Bruhier, and we can go over the Dragon Dominion. But not the Low Forest. If you want to get to the Northwestern Lands, you'll have to travel there by foot."

I let out a sigh. My face must have shown my disappointment because she relented.

"Look, I'll tell you what I can do. I can't take you all the way to the desert, because I can't fly over the Low Forest. But if you want, I'll take you as far as the final mountain range separating the Dragon Dominion from the desert. But no further."

"That would be very helpful." Relief made my voice crack from the strain I'd been putting on it from holding my breath. "Can you take us now?"

She shook her head. "No, not tonight. I have some things to tie up. Morning is best for us to leave anyway, especially if we are flying over the mountains. We'll leave at daybreak if you're sure you want my crew to take you."

I didn't want to chance losing her sudden change of heart, so I bit back my impatience and smiled. "That's fine. Tomorrow is fine." I paused, looking at her magnificent airship before turned back at her. Something she'd mentioned had piqued my curiosity. "You mentioned no one knows why you can't fly over the Low Forest. So how exactly does the ship run?"

She rolled one shoulder dismissively. "No one really knows specifics. It's all magic, but I'm sure a smart Librarian already knows that bit. The propellers, rudders, and other navigational things are similar to water ships. All I know about flight and lift is magic makes it happen. The problem with the Low Forest is whatever magic keeps us aloft seems to become completely nullified the minute we cross into it."

Gwen stepped forward. "What do you mean, nullified? What would happen if you tried?"

Her face became solemn. "I've only seen it once, but once was enough for me to know the limits of an airship and never attempt it myself. When I was a young ship hand, long before I had my own vessel, another shipmaster challenged my ship to a race. To the mountain range and back; a mere lark during some downtime between jobs.

"But something happened with their steering, or perhaps a rudder or propeller, I'm still not sure." She shook her head, pressing her lips together for a moment, she paused before continuing. "We watched as it passed over the final mountain range, then instantly plummeted, free-falling straight down, where it crashed to the rocks below. We searched for survivors, but no one made it. By the time we'd landed in a safe place and trekked up to the crash site, a few hours later, all hands were lost."

I gulped. If I'd wanted to argue, beseech, or cajole her past her limits this story gave me adequate pause. For our own sakes, as well as hers, nothing would induce me to push her limits further now I'd heard this.

"I'm sorry, I didn't know. I can't imagine how difficult it must have been for you," I offered hesitantly.

She took a deep breath and brushed off my concern. "It was many years ago. I tell you this story not for sympathy, but so you can understand I'm not saying no to be difficult." She smiled suddenly. "If I was able to fix a ship so I could go into the Low Forest, imagine how much money I'd make. Why, I'd have a monopoly!" She added a wink, causing the guys to chuckle in response.

I looked at Gwen to see what she thought.

She'd been quiet the entire time and had an odd look on her face.

When I tilted my head and raised my eyebrows, she shook her head slightly and smoothed out her expression. I didn't press for her thoughts, deciding I'd ask later. It seemed important, although I wasn't sure if it was related to our mission or something else.

It felt like we had a lot of catching up to do when we could catch a quiet moment.

"I'm assuming you have enough money for this trip?"

Baeley turned to Will in a businesslike fashion, interrupting my train of thought.

He nodded, handing her a pouch of gold coins about the same size as the one he'd given her on our previous trip.

She opened the sack, counted it, and nodded. "Perfect. You can put your belongings aboard now, just make sure to stay out of the way of the deckhands and make yourself scarce. We'll leave first thing in the morning. You can use the same bunk as last time, and spend the night if you want, unless you find better lodgings elsewhere, which I'd recommend if you want anything plush."

He gave a gallant bow, smiling as he stood. "The bunks will be wonderful. Lovely to do business with you. We'll be ready and eager to depart first thing."

She shook her head as she looked at us with amusement. "You're all becoming quite the adventurers. Who knows, maybe someday, you'll want to take a post as part of my crew. You seem like a rather good lot, crazy, if not perhaps overtly brave. And the skinny boy at the back looks like he's in love with the whole flying thing."

Sel's eyes widened at being addressed, touching a tentative hand to his chest.

She snorted. "Yeah, you kid. I've been watching you. I think you've got the makings of a decent airman. But obviously something to think about later, as you're on your own mission. Now if you'll excuse me, I've work to do."

She tipped her hat, turned on her heel, and strode away.

As I watched her return to the ship and begin to bark orders, I couldn't keep my mind from returning to thoughts about the magic able to power an airship, as well as Gwen's mysterious look.

We had a lot of catching up to do, and though I was frustrated at the delay in departure, part of me was happy I'd have a chance to talk to her privately before we left. I had a feeling our conversation would change my life in some unknown fashion.

CHAPTER 7

We stored unnecessary items in the bunk and headed back to town to blow off some steam.

Gwen needed items for the wolves, since she hadn't had much luck with hunting on the side of the mountain other than for small ptarmigan like the one we'd shared earlier.

I'd put my odorous change of clothing down and seriously considered buying another change of clothing. I wasn't sure the smell would ever come out or if I could find replacements, but I was eager to throw the ones I had away.

Gwen paused as we walked down the gangplank, so I gently tugged on her arm. She turned, uncertainty filling her beautiful eyes along with something which looked suspiciously like tears.

"What is it? Why do you look so sad?" I pulled her close, hoping the contact would cheer her up. "You know Baeley and the other shipmates love your wolves. And they look far more comfortable this time. They're not even curled up on the bunk but roaming the ship like they own it. I may or may not have seen the good captain slip Swift a piece of meat from her own lunch."

She gave me a watery smile. "I know they're fine, I mean,

they don't spend all their time with me. I'm just uncomfortable. This far from home, I'm feeling unusually uncertain and I don't like it."

I gave her a quick hug. "You've got me. And the boys, if they count." I rolled my eyes, earning a realistic chuckle this time. "Come on, we don't have much time. Will knows a market which he swears has what you need for Swift and the others, and I need a new change of clothes."

She pulled away, giving me an exaggerated sniff. "That you do, my friend, that you do."

I mock-glared at her, and we both burst into laughter.

The others were walking ahead and turned to see what was so funny, which only made us laugh harder. We caught up with them but didn't bother to quench their curiosity.

"You mentioned there's a market?" I worked to stifle my giggles with some difficulty.

Will narrowed his eyes as he regarded me. "Yeah, not too far from here. Were you looking for something specific, or just for her wolves?"

I nodded, sniffing my tunic, and wrinkling my nose. "Yeah, actually. I think this attire is on the verge of needing to be burnt to ward off evil. Unless there's a way to decontaminate the things I'm wearing aboard the ship, I wouldn't mind buying one or two changes of clothing to replace what I've been wearing."

His ready agreement irritated me even though I'd invited it. "Yeah, there should be a clothier with ready-made stuff in the market. Due to their proximity to the docks, they get a lot of travelers."

He inclined his head to the left and we followed him.

As promised, the small marketplace had everything we needed.

Gwen found meat for her wolves, which Sel offered to carry. She accepted gratefully. It was nice of him, but I had a tough time looking away from his scrawny form carrying the huge sack. He hardly seemed big enough, but he didn't complain.

I purchased a change of clothing on sale, which thrilled me more than I'd expected. I'd never cared about what I wore before, but I guess even a book lover appreciated clothes when they were required.

Once we'd finished getting the necessities, we stood around and stared at each other awkwardly.

"Now what?" I looked between them, waiting for an idea. "We have a few hours left. Do we want to find a place to stay in town? Or would you like to sleep on the ship?"

Sel readjusted the weight of the meat on his back. "If it's all the same with you, Rhin, since you're with Will *and* Gwen, would you be okay if I went back to the ship?" He gave a sheepish smile. "I'll take the meat back for the wolves. I'd like to spend more time on the ship, learning more about the life of a flying man. Of course, if you need me..." he hastily tried to downplay his request, but I raised my hand.

"No, it's fine. You go on back to the ship. Can you take my new clothing back too? You're sure you'll be okay?" I looked around the marketplace after passing the items over. It was a bustling, vibrant place, without any concerning individuals loitering and the sun would be up for a few more hours. Nothing to make me think he wouldn't be okay, but I worried anyway. He was so young still.

"Yes, I'll be fine. Will you be returning tonight?" He tried to sound politely uninterested, but the hopeful expression on his face gave him away.

A brief look at the other two confirmed my thoughts. "I think it's best we do. I don't want to chance missing our flight in the morning. Sunrise can be hard to predict when you're fast asleep."

"And we've already paid our fare, which means tonight's lodgings are basically free."

Will pointed at Gwen. "Right on the money. If you'd like,

we could test out the nightlife, in controlled measure, of course."

Sel raised his eyebrows, laughed at Will's rakish smile, turned, and waved as he headed back toward the docks.

I watched him walk away with fond amusement, knowing he thought we were about to get out of control. I'd say he should know me better, but as I was continually discovering new facets of my personality on this journey, maybe his concerns were something to keep in mind. Especially if we wanted to make sure we were on board with him and the wolves in the morning.

Before I could reply to Will's offer, Gwen chimed in.

"I'd love to see a little of the nightlife. Do you know any good places? I could go for a nice dinner and a few drinks to relax." She looked at me, eyes wide with hope. "What do you say, Rhin?"

It was clear she wanted me to be on board. I smiled at her eagerness. "Sure. But I don't want to be out late. Staying out all night is just as bad as missing the ship in the morning because we slept in."

Will put a hand over his heart. "I solemnly promise to return you to the ship before midnight. Milady's?" He held his elbows out to accept our arms.

I snorted but accepted one arm while she took the other. Sel was long gone, having turned the corner a few moments earlier.

It was just the three of us now. I felt lighthearted, but also strangely unsettled. I'd been holding Gwen's arm until now as we'd rambled through the market and his was a poor substitute.

He was objectively quite attractive for a human, but he was a little too cocky for my taste, and sometimes seemed to go out of his way to poke at me. Kind of like a brother, who spent most of his time deliberately trying to get a rise out of me.

Besides, I still needed to get Gwen alone and talk to her,

which his presence got in the way of. Hopefully, I'd get a chance tonight, before we returned to the ship.

"Ladies first." He held the door of a nearby building open.

I looked up to see a sign, *the Barmy Badger.*

"I'm not sure the name of this establishment is promising when it comes to food quality," I muttered.

Gwen snickered as he looked down, affronted.

"I'll have you know they only serve the *best* barmy badgers." His voice rang with mock indignity.

I still had my doubts, but from the size of the patrons, it would likely be filling, if nothing else. The first thing I noticed as I stepped over the threshold was a clean establishment smelling of delicious food. It wasn't fancy, but it was packed. Always a good sign.

We snagged a table along an unoccupied wall. We didn't have to wait long before a tavern maid came to take our order.

She was a matronly woman who reminded me a little of Marthe, just lacking her warmth and about twenty years younger.

"What'll you have?" She crossed her arms, a bored but pleasant expression on her lined face.

I looked at my friends before turning back to the woman. "Do you have any specials tonight, ma'am? It smells delicious in here and we're quite hungry."

The woman quickly rattled off the day's special.

I held a hand up for one, and Will and Gwen seconded my order.

We added on a pitcher of the house ale and waited for the food without speaking.

I was too busy looking around to feel like chatting, impressed by how similar one tavern could look to another. Considering this was only the second such place I'd been in, I'd expected it to look different. But other than a slightly different location for the bar along a wall instead of in the center, it was almost identical.

Once the food arrived, we dug in, a hearty, companionable silence continuing until the fervor of eating had calmed.

Will leaned back in his chair, placing his mug on the table, and let out a satisfied burp.

Gwen and I glared disapprovingly until he apologized, albeit without any real remorse.

He leaned forward again, resting both elbows on the table and his chin on his fists. "Any idea what you'd like to get up to tonight?" His eyes sparkled. "Want to see if we can stir up trouble?"

Gwen scoffed. "Hardly! Supper and a relaxing drink are pretty much what I'm in the mood for. The last few weeks have been … challenging, to say the least."

He agreed. "True. I'm not even sure I'll have a job to go back to after this. Although my sergeant was okay with the idea of allowing me to go along with you guys for protection, I'm not sure he anticipated I'd be gone this long."

"I'm sorry, I hope you do." I grimaced at the thought he'd lose his job, but he waved an airy hand.

"Don't worry about it. With the way things are shaping up in Lynia, it's either go with you and see if I can keep you from injuring yourselves, or get sent to the front, where ur'gel are taking out men by the score."

Just like that, the mood shifted from giddy to solemn.

Gwen turned to me. "Have you heard anything about the Cliffs?"

I shook my head, shoulders slumping as I considered my family. "No, no word. I'm not even sure anyone is alive."

Will's normally mocking, slightly irritating expression became unexpectedly sympathetic. "I'm sure everyone's okay. I don't know the area well but from what I understand, the Cliffs are very well fortified. It's unlikely even an attack by a full army of ur'gel would be able to completely decimate them. In Sunglen, within the human military, elves are respected as some of the toughest and most tenacious fighters in Lynia."

I smiled, touched he cared enough about my feelings to try to reassure me. "Thanks. I worry about them, but I know the best way to ensure everyone is safe, and no one else's family's subjected to attack the way mine was, is to trap Dag'draath back in his kennel. Or put him in a better kennel, one sturdy enough to last longer than a few centuries."

Gwen took a swig of her ale, slamming the mug down on the table. "Hear, hear!" She cheered, slightly louder than necessary.

I looked around, but no one was paying us any attention. The tavern had emptied since we'd arrived and was now only half full, and the other patrons didn't even look up.

I returned to the conversation. "Hopefully, if we find the Heart Stone where it was last seen this will all be over, and we can be home before the next high holidays." I half-heartedly raised my glass, taking a sip, wishing I believed my own words.

Will joined my toast, holding up his mug as well. "From your mouth to Suun's ears."

We raised our glasses again, but once Will had taken a sip, he looked at us and wiggled his eyebrows.

"I'll be back in a few minutes. Nature calls."

I bit back a laugh at her raised eyebrow, but as he left, I realized this was my chance. Now was the perfect moment to ask about the mysterious look on her face back at the docks. But before I could speak, she cleared her throat and turned to me.

Her eyes were wide, cheeks flushed, and the same look on her face again. "There's something I've been trying to find a way to tell you, but I'm not sure how to begin."

I moved closer, eager to know what was making her look so conflicted. "What? You can tell me anything. Don't worry, I'm sure there's nothing you can say that would ever make me think less of you."

Her flush deepened, traveling from her face down her throat. "I'm glad. That's just it, you... Well, you're the first loyal friend I've ever had who wasn't a wolf. I never fit in with other elves, even as a kid. What I feel for you goes deeper than friendship, but I don't want to mess that up, either, because I really value it. I mean..."

She stopped, letting out a frustrated growl as she tugged on a lock of her long golden hair as if it had suddenly made her mad. Her mouth worked for a few moments, and I placed a hand on top of hers in concern.

She looked at me, instantly still.

"It's okay. I mean, you're my best friend, too." I shrugged, giving her a rueful smile. "You know I've never fit in with the Cliff Elves, either. We're two outcasts, making a family in our own way."

Her eyes softened and she moved closer. My eyes widened as I looked at her, unable to pull away from the mesmerizing expression I still couldn't quite read.

"I think... I mean, I know... I'm sure I'm falling in love with you." Her words left in a rush and I froze, able only to stare.

I realized I was close enough to feel her sweetly scented breath on my cheek. She leaned in, and for the first time, our lips met. It was soft and light, barely more than the brush of her warm mouth against mine.

In my shock and bewilderment, I neither responded nor pulled away. I was unsure what to do next and before I could react, she had already broken the kiss.

Her eyes sparkled over cheeks flushed a fiery red. She lowered her eyes and pushed back her chair. It scraped loudly against the scarred wooden floor like an attack alarm, and without a word, she bolted from the table.

CHAPTER 8

"What just happened?" The sound of Will's confused voice penetrated my fog.

I looked at him, blinking for a moment before I shrugged. I was helpless to describe the swirl of emotions and put the situation into words for someone else.

"I'm not sure. I think I just ruined everything. She just told me she..." My words trailed off as I tried to process her words before the kiss.

He sat down, his smirking and all-knowing expression firmly back in place. "I see. So, Gwen of the Wolves finally took the plunge and told you how she feels? I'm gathering from the fact she just took off out the back, probably looking for a fight, your answer wasn't all she'd hoped."

I looked at him, stunned. "You knew she liked me?"

He sat down, raising a shoulder nonchalantly, taking a sip of his beer. "Oh yeah, don't get me wrong, it's not because I'm insightful or anything. I think it's probably obvious to everybody, but you, she's been carrying a torch for you."

I shook my head in disbelief. "How is this possible? I mean, I thought we were just friends. She's my best friend, but I had no idea she ... loved me."

"What can I say? The heart wants what the heart wants." He gave me a commiserating smile, holding his glass up in a salute as what happened finally sank in.

"I just... I mean, I thought she, you, well, you know. When you guys left me in Starside..." I flinched as he burst into laughter.

"Okay, really? How could you think she was interested in me? You don't remember the time she punched me in the nose and made it bleed everywhere?" He mimed blood flying out of his nose, "I mean, yeah, of course, I'm attractive, and who wouldn't want to be with me? But believe me when I say, if anyone out there could resist my charms it's her."

Out of nowhere, a bubble of hysterical laughter spilled out of me.

His eyebrows raised, "Are you okay? Was that odd squeak the final thread of your sanity snapping?"

I swatted blindly at him, not actually trying to make contact, but delaying a response until I was able to respond in a semi-intelligent manner.

"It never crossed my mind she felt like that. I don't think anyone's ever cared about me before. Male or female."

I sighed, staring into my half-empty glass as I remembered the look on her face as she'd rushed off.

It had been hurt.

I had deeply hurt her without even trying. Which was the very last thing I ever wanted to do.

Will leaned over the table, patting my hand. "Cheer up. It's not like you've done anything irreparable. I don't think." He added, grimacing when I looked up. "I mean, it's pretty natural to be confused when you're as clueless to the emotions of others as you've always seemed to be."

"Hey!" I pulled my hand back and glared at him.

He assumed a sleepy look. "Let's face it. You're a great gal, but you spend all your time with your nose in a book. It's not surprising you didn't realize your friend wanted to be more.

Besides, there's nothing wrong with it. Lots of people are clueless. And don't try to tell me you don't feel anything for her. I've watched you two together. Sickeningly sweet."

"I don't understand. We're just friends. Well, I thought we were." I dropped my head to my hands, trying to puzzle out how everything had gotten messed up so fast.

He shook his head, taking my chin and tilting it up to see a patient, bittersweet look on his face. "No, Rhin, you aren't just friends. I don't know how long you've known each other, but from the first time I met you in Sunglen I could see you'd die to keep each other safe. I've got a lot of friends, and I'd do my best for them, but I don't think I'm willing to die for them. My mother, yes. But not my friends. Sacrificing yourself, especially for people who appreciate logic over emotion, is something you only do for family, or someone you love."

I swallowed and leaned back in my chair as I considered his words. Was he right? Did I have feelings for Gwen? I thought back over the time since I'd met her, and how every time I'd been outside the castle, I'd sought her out.

I'd always thought it was because we were friends, but looking back, I realized I'd always felt a tingle of excitement and warmth and looked forward to seeing her in a way I didn't with any other friend. Or family, for that matter. Maybe he knew something I didn't.

Will waved a hand in front of my face. "Hello? Is Rhin home? You've been practically catatonic for the last few minutes. Either the ale is finally hitting you, or my first assumption was correct."

I let out a weak chuckle. "No, I'm just thinking about your words. It's possible you're right. But as the idea never crossed my mind before, it's taking some time to process." I shrugged, feeling the need to apologize. "I always thought I liked the male gender until now."

"No, you're drawn to someone who's competent and brave. You appreciate someone who doesn't care about what other people think or let others make their decisions for them. Someone who's smart, funny, and kind. There's a reason you wanted her to travel with you, even though from what I understand, before the journey you mostly had an intermittent, long-distance friendship."

It made so much sense to me now. I didn't know how I hadn't seen it before. "You're right. I told myself I wanted her to come with me because she was capable and probably knew how to get to Sunglen better than I did. But if I'd been looking for a guide, I could have asked my brother, or even one of the older elves."

He lifted a hand, palm-up. "See? Now you're thinking."

"I asked her to come because I wanted to be with her, didn't I?" I sighed, unable to comprehend how blind I'd been.

He leaned back, taking another sip out of his mug. Giving me a satisfied smile, he nodded. "Now you're onto the truth, Princess. So, what are you gonna do about it?"

CHAPTER 9

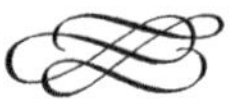

I polished off my drink and headed out the way I'd seen Gwen leave. Buoyed by Will's surprisingly sensible advice, I knew I needed to make sure she wasn't dealing with her emotions by getting into a fight.

She was everything Will said she was; brave, tough, kind, and funny, but I was worried because in a fit of emotion, she may have bitten off more than she could chew.

When we found her leaning over, resting her hands on her knees as she caught her breath near a refuse pile, I knew he'd been correct. Apparently, even though I had more education, Will was far more adept in the art of reading others. Then again, who wasn't?

"Gwen?"

We approached slowly, like she was a wild animal who could lash out any second.

I was nervous around her in a way I'd never been before. I couldn't believe I'd been so blind and hurt her feelings so badly or been so unaware of my own feelings. I knew whatever conversation happened next would need to be initiated by me, I just wasn't sure what the best thing to say was.

She flipped her hair back, looking stoic and tough. I

winced when I saw the abrasion on one high cheekbone, a small trickle of blood leaking from her nose. Her eyes widened as they met mine, then narrowed into an expressionless pool, betraying nothing of her emotions.

I exhaled, disappointed she wasn't in the mood to talk, but relieved she was mostly in one piece. "Are you okay?"

I stopped a few yards away, glancing back to see Will had paused as well.

He stood just to my left, with his hands loosely clasped behind his back while he rocked on his heels, as though waiting in line for a show, but wisely out of range of her fist. I guess once was enough for him and he wasn't taking any chances.

She lifted her chin, sniffed once as she wiped away another small trickle of blood, and stood up. "Yup. Everything's fine."

I searched her face, her eyes, looking for a sign of any sort that would tell me what I needed to do next. But she wore the face of a stranger. As much as it pained me to drop it, now clearly wasn't the time to press. The sun had been down for a few hours, and with the excitement and confusion of the evening decreasing to a smolder, I was fatigued from the long day of hiking and unexpected emotional turmoil.

"Oh." I cleared my throat and tried again. "Well, I guess we should head back to the ship." I bit my lip, turning to Will, silently pleading for him to do something.

He merely unclasped his hands. "Sounds good. You'll be pleased to know I paid on our way out, so no one from the tavern should be following us." He arched an eyebrow as he looked her up and down, "As long as whatever caused your sudden change in appearance has been taken care of?"

She abruptly finished brushing herself off and turned away. "Let's go."

The trip back to the ship was silent, but not the same companionable silence I'd always enjoyed when traveling with her in the past. This was a silence that stretched between two continents, yawning wide with an ocean of unvoiced apologies and unspoken emotions. It was treacherous to traverse, but necessary to bridge if those continents would ever be at home beside each other again.

Captain Baeley was on deck as we climbed the gangplank. She gave us a cheery nod. "Well here's an earlier evening than I expected. After speaking with young Sel over there, I assumed you'd be out carousing all night."

She gestured toward the mid-mast, where he was listening to a deckhand beside the mid-mast with a rapt expression on his face.

Will shrugged but didn't divulge any details about what had been the most important, as well as troublesome, part of our night.

"We're tired is all. We just had a nice meal at *the Barmy Badger,* a pint of ale, and felt it best to head back and sleep in the bunks. A good night's sleep prior to liftoff and all. Unless, of course, there's something you'd like us to do prior to turning in for the night?" He waited politely, earning a smile and shake of the head from her in return.

"No, go on to bed. Perhaps these two young elves have been a good influence on you after all, my young soldier-friend. The boy I knew a few weeks ago would likely have missed the ship." She spoke mildly, but I could hear the amusement in her voice.

He brushed off the mild censure, giving her a broad smile as he slouched past her. "People change, captain, people change."

He sauntered by without a care in the world, but Gwen and I paused at her assessing look.

"Is everything all right?" Her eyes had narrowed as she took in Gwen's injuries, but she shook her head.

"Everything's perfect." Gwen's voice was flat and gave away nothing.

The captain nodded without comment as Gwen brushed

past, leaving me behind to follow her with my eyes. When I focused back on Captain Baeley, she'd raised her eyebrows and was watching me with interest. "How about you, Princess?"

I bristled, feeling defensive but kept my reply simple. "Yeah, we're fine. Gwen got into a scuffle, I guess. But she assured us no one's coming after her, so everything should be fine."

I could hear the glumness in my tone and tried to camouflage it with a smile. Before I could catch up to the others, she gave me a light slap on the shoulder.

"Buck up, Rhin. I've seen that look before. I have a feeling this flight may be a bit more of an education than you expect." She turned back to what she'd been working when we'd entered the ship.

I sighed, not certain I wanted to know what she meant, and headed below deck.

AS IT TURNED OUT, even though Captain Baeley was unable to take us all the way to the Northwestern Lands, the distance to the far mountain range even by airship was lengthy, so her assistance would cut days, if not weeks, off our journey. If I'd thought at one point making it from Cliffside to Sunglen was a challenge, once I'd sat down to examine our route on the maps aboard the ship, I realized how small an adventure our previous trip had been.

At least the book on dragon history was turning out to be extremely helpful, and I was determined to know everything I could about the land we were journeying to. Everything I found in the book led me to believe something had changed significantly, since they were written only a few hundred years earlier. The description of the region past the mountains of the Dragon Dominion was a fertile, bountiful paradise, which struck me as odd. Whenever I spoke with anyone who'd been there recently, it was far from the case.

I couldn't help but suspect Dag'draath had something to do with it and redoubled my efforts to find the resting place of the Heart Stone. Of course, this meant I was spending most of my time with my nose in a book, as I'd been accused of doing earlier.

Relations between Gwen and myself remained strained. I kept waiting for an opening, but she was monosyllabic and chose to spend a lot of her time with the wolves below deck.

For the most part I could tell she and the wolves had gotten over their initial fear of flying, so I knew she was avoiding me.

It crushed me in many ways. Firstly, because I'd wounded her so deeply, we couldn't even enjoy our previous friendship, and secondly, with the absence of her companionship, I truly realized how much I cared for her in return.

I knew fixing the rift could be as easy as telling her, but every time I worked up the courage, she left or someone else was around. It never seemed to be the right time and finding her was half the struggle.

On the third morning of our flight, I woke up early. When I found everyone else still sleeping in their bunks, I headed above deck with my satchel and books to get some fresh air and hopefully, some breakfast.

Above deck, there was only a skeleton crew at that hour of day, so when I spotted a large object off to the ship's port-side, I was justifiably concerned.

Luckily, at the same moment, Captain Baeley appeared at her station.

"Captain Baeley, what's that, over there?"

She squinted to where I pointed, and her face tightened. Instead of answering, she strode across the deck, whispered something into the ear of the mizzen mate, who scrambled up the mid-mast as quickly as one of the small animals in the Low Forest climbed a tree.

My concern was quickly turning to alarm, even though I couldn't help but be impressed by the ease with which the

D'ahvol man moved. It was a good argument for why elves and humans made good matches when it came to offspring, not the drivel I frequently heard back home.

She turned to me and smiled. "Good eye, Princess." She raised an eyebrow. "You'd make a good spotter. You ever been up top?"

I followed her gaze toward the lookout post, high above the ship, and felt a little dizzy. "No, I haven't."

She nodded, biting her lip as her eyes bored into me.

I began to feel self-conscious, my skin prickling as though she was trying to somehow look under it and read my inner thoughts. But her gaze softened, and I brushed the strange thought aside until she spoke.

"Well, it seems like something we should probably rectify."

I swallowed hard, gesturing in the direction I'd seen the dark object to deflect her. "I'd like that sometime. But what is that thing? What did I see?"

She rolled her eyes, her face resuming her usual, easy-going expression.

"Ah, just a few dragons. Don't worry. My crew know what to do about them. We shouldn't be bothered too much."

I turned to look for the dark object again, but whatever I'd seen was out of sight. I cocked my head to the side as I looked at her. "Dragons? Are they usually a problem?"

"From time to time they like to see our airships up close. They can be a nuisance, but we're well equipped to deal with them. I haven't lost any passengers ... yet." She winked.

I opened my mouth, ready to question her further when a crew member shouted from behind us. She turned on her heel and jogged over. The shipmate hadn't sounded frightened and as I no longer saw what I assumed was the dragon, I headed to my favorite reading spot to do more research.

"Hey, how's everything going?"

I blinked, realizing my neck was stiff, and my eyes were scratchy. I took a moment to stretch, before turning to smile at

Will. He'd already assumed his usual nonchalant position of leaning against the deck railing, but he was looking at my book with interest.

"Good, I think." I flipped through the pages, holding up a picture of the area. "This is where we're going."

The picture I'd chosen was one which highlighted the lush greenery of the area. "Apparently, not long ago, this place used to be some sort of paradise. A place where edible harvests abounded, and hunting was rich. Sometime after this narrative was written, it turned into the desert we now know as the Northwestern Lands."

I narrowed my eyes, still trying to shape the ill-formed ideas running through my head.

"I think it has something to do with what happened during the Dark War. Perhaps it was all the battles they had tearing up the land, but I'm wondering if it happened when Suun trapped Dag'draath."

"Could be. I'd imagine a spell with enough juice to trap a god would take a great deal of energy, even for another god."

"Exactly what I was thinking. What if the reason it's a desert now is because of the energy cost? We all know magic takes a lot of energy from either the practitioner, Lynia, or both. Maybe the prison is breaking because the energy is almost used up."

"Hmmm, sounds logical." He winked at me and I looked away.

My cheeks felt warm. Was I was blushing? I wasn't used to people praising anything I did. I forced myself to ignore my self-consciousness and looked around. No one else was nearby, so I quickly changed the subject.

"Is anyone else awake?" I tried to keep my voice light, but his knowing look told me I hadn't fooled him.

"No, Gwen and the wolves are still sleeping, and I think Sel may have found a nest of hornets to snuggle, given the noises I can hear coming from him."

I chuckled, remembering the loud snoring which had woken me this morning. "Can I ask you something?"

He plopped down beside me on the bench before I could say another word. "About Gwen?" His voice was strangely soft.

I nodded, certain my frustration and sadness were as obvious as I thought they were. "Yeah, I don't know what to do."

"Well, the first step is to figure out what you want to do. How do you feel about the idea of having a relationship with her?"

"Honestly? I think it's what I want. But I haven't had a chance to even speak with her since we boarded. Here we are, basically trapped on a ship together with neither of us able to escape, and every time I try to have a conversation with her, she runs away or makes sure somebody else is around." I could hear the petulant whine in my voice and winced. "I must sound childish to you."

He snorted. "Not at all. Look, I'm no expert on matters of the heart, but I think you need to keep trying. She's a lot softer than she appears."

When I drew my eyebrows together, unsure where he was going with his line of thinking, he shook his head. I heard a trace of laughter in his voice now.

"Not physically softer. I mean, for all she comes across as tough, her heart is far more tender than yours. You have a toughness, a kind of single-mindedness about you I don't recognize in her. She may be prone to fits of anger or fighting when threatened…"

I knew we were both thinking of the fight at the tavern before we departed. "She does like to fight."

I smirked as he touched his nose before nodding.

"But a lot of the physical acting out she does is because she's not sure how to express her emotions, any more than you are. It took a great deal of courage for her to tell you she cared in the first place. I think she's probably used up her supply for now." He hesitated, as if debating whether to tell me, then spoke in a rush. "You may have to push her. And what I mean is you may have to take her aside and spell it out for her. Because I have a feeling she's going to avoid you until the end of the trip, even if she sticks around to help."

My shoulders slumped under the heavy weight I'd been carrying since the tavern. It felt like it had been hovering and now was firmly on top of me, squeezing the air out of my chest.

He was right.

I would have to show her. I'd already known the next move would have to be mine, but it would have to be something impressive to get past the wall of brooding she'd erected between us.

"What should I do?" I hoped he had some ideas, because I was stumped. "What would you do if you needed to apologize to someone you had feelings for?"

"I've never really had that issue." He wiggled his eyebrows. "All I have to do is flash a smile and tell them they're attractive and I've had no problems."

At my look of disappointment, he relented.

"Really, I've never been in your position. I've either known from the start somebody was into me or been the one to end things."

I exhaled, wishing as I did the weight would fly away with it. I forced a smile I didn't feel. "Thanks anyway. I think I have some work to do. Who knows? Maybe I'll read something helpful."

He clapped me on the back and stood just as she came on deck, followed by Swift. He shot me a wink, turning toward Captain Baeley, who was standing at the stern.

When Gwen saw me, I watched her steps falter. She adjusted her trajectory just enough she headed away from me, giving me a slight wave of acknowledgment before heading to look over the side, as if she'd planned to go there all along.

Reluctantly, I picked my book up again. It didn't look like this morning was going to be my chance to make amends either.

I'd only managed to read a few pages when the soft warmth of fur against my leg caused me to look down. Swift was sitting beside me, looking at me with an expression I could only describe as curious.

I smiled, greeting him by burying my face in his fur with a wave of sadness. "Good morning, Swift. She's still mad at me, isn't she?" I drew back like I thought he would respond. I knew he was just a wolf, but the look he gave me was so patient and sympathetic it made me feel he understood.

At first, I'd thought Gwen was with him, but I could now see he'd wandered over while she was speaking with one of the crew. She still stood in the same spot she'd been when I'd picked up my book.

I looked down again, keeping my voice low. "It would be wonderful if you could tell me how to apologize and tell her I care about her, too. I never meant to hurt her feelings. I was just so surprised I didn't have a chance to find the words before she ran away. And now she won't have anything to do with me."

Swift didn't answer, but pressed his head more firmly into my side, as though he was hugging me back. The warmth of his fur gave me hope. Even though she wasn't looking at me, I felt my resolve strengthen.

I knew I would do whatever it took to tell her how I felt. After all, if Will thought I was hardhearted, surely, I could handle a little bit of a bruise to that organ, if it meant a chance at achieving true love and getting my friend back.

CHAPTER 10

My resolve was tested almost immediately. Shortly after the realization I was willing to fight for her love, Swift trotted back to Gwen.

She'd patted him with a strange look on her face, glancing at me beneath her lashes. My cheeks flushed and I looked down at the book instead of meeting her eyes.

I realized I'd been staring at the page without turning it for far too long and shut the book. Steeling myself to meet her cold eyes, I looked up only to find she'd vanished. I scanned the deck, but she wasn't anywhere. Disappointment bitter in my mouth, I stared at the last place I'd seen her and completely missed Captain Baeley coming up behind me.

"All right, I wasn't going to say anything." She spoke boldly and I looked up, surprised at her presence and the tone of her voice.

"Excuse me? About what?"

She sat next to me, gesturing at the emptiness beside me, where the ghost of Gwen still lingered.

"About her. Anyone can see you two are made for each other. So, I want to know what happened between you two in the time between you asking me for a ride and returning from the tavern. Something big must've gone down at *the Barmy Badger* to cause a rift as wide as the distance between Bruhier and the Low Forest." She watched me with an uncomfortable shrewdness.

My gaze slid away. I tried to compose something logical she'd believe, but when I looked back, I knew I wouldn't be able to pull anything over on her wise, experienced eyes. I got the feeling she could spot a lie from a mile away. Just like Will, she was obviously a far better judge of emotions and social behavior than I.

"I hurt Gwen's feelings." At her raised eyebrows, I hastened to clarify what I meant. "It wasn't intentional. I wouldn't have hurt her, I don't think, if I'd been prepared."

I exhaled, looking at my empty hands laying limp in my lap. I couldn't help but think if I hadn't screwed up, they might be holding Gwen's right now.

Captain Baeley chuckled dryly. "So that's the way of it. I thought as much."

She sounded upbeat but I could tell she wasn't laughing at me, more at a remembered event from her own life. Her eyes were warm but had a wistful look, and hope grew in my chest. Maybe she'd know what to say to fix this. After all, she was a woman, too.

"Will told me what I'd done, even before we left the tavern, and I've been trying to find a way to apologize ever since. But she won't have anything to do with me. I'm not sure I can fix the damage before she has a chance to leave. I'll never see her again." I sniffed, the hot prickle of tears of disappointment and sorrow desperately trying to punch their way out.

She put her arm around me and gave me a tight, motherly hug.

"It feels like that now, but these are the early days yet." She turned, moving so both of her strong hands gripped my shoulders. As she looked into my eyes, conviction shone clearly out. "If you want to get her back, you're going to need to fight for her. It's not like in a book, where you learn about some glorious history of people long ago, or even a book people invent where everything has a happy ending. You're a Librarian. You need to be the hero of your own story if you hope to work this out."

I shook my head. It was hopeless. "It's not that easy. I've never had feelings for anyone before and I've never messed up someone else's declaration of love. If only I'd been quicker on my feet, or could go back in time and fix..." I trailed off, unable to find words to express my disappointment and despair.

Her face remained unchanged. "Look, you're a Librarian. That means something around these parts. Librarians are more than mere keepers of books and histories. You need to be more than someone who reads and stockpiles information. A Librarian protects knowledge. They decide who gets to have it, and more. They are warriors, explorers, and adventurers."

I shook my head, knowing she was talking about more than just a relationship, but not understanding. "What does my being a Librarian have to do with getting Gwen back? I mean, it's not why she loves me, or why she's upset. So how can being a Librarian help?"

To my surprise, she winked. "Look, Princess, I've had more than one Librarian aboard my ship over the years. Every single one of them had the kind of grit and steel you don't find around every corner. I know you have it in you, but I'm not sure *you* do. So, what are you going to do about your situation?"

I shrugged against her almost uncomfortably tight grip.

She removed her hands and sat back, leaning against the back of the bench as she observed me without speaking. The silence stretched out, becoming awkward by the time I realized she was waiting for me to come up with an idea.

"The only idea I have is to find her and tell her I'm sorry. But she won't even let me do that. I think I need a grand gesture, but what can I do on a ship? My options are limited, even if I can manage to get her alone."

Her face lit up, and a sly smile spread across her face. "You want to know what to do on a ship? Follow me. I've got something to show you." She stood up and began walking. When it looked like she had no intention of waiting, I shoved my books in my satchel and raced after her.

"Wow."

I felt as though I was in a whole new world. If being aboard an airship wasn't magical enough, when she took me up to the crow's nest and I looked out, it was as though I was the only living creature in the world. I was floating in the clouds. Without being able to see any part of the ship around me as I looked out, I felt minuscule, yet simultaneously powerful. I turned to her; positive she could see how awed I was when she started chuckling.

"Exactly. Most people I've brought up here have been flabbergasted, much as you are right now. I know Gwen was frightened when she first boarded the ship, but she's a brave girl and it settled. I have a feeling this may be the trick. Here's what I propose."

I leaned in closer, trying to catch every word. It was oddly loud so high up as the gulls shrieked over the water.

She continued. "Based on your own admission, pretty much everybody has more experience with matters of the heart than you do. So, if I was trying to impress someone, what I'd do is bring them up here and create a private picnic. Once you're alone with your captive audience, you can pour your heart out and let her know how sorry you are."

I blinked for a moment as her words sank in, realizing once they had how perfect her idea was. Before I could stop myself, I'd thrown myself at her spontaneously, hugging a woman I hardly knew. I pulled back quickly, grateful she wasn't upset based on her peals of laughter.

We sat there a while longer, troubleshooting my glorious plan for redemption. Things moved as though time had become fluid, strangely fast, yet slow. As part of her amazing idea to win Gwen over, she allowed me to bother the cook, even giving instructions on what to ask for. Once I packed the picnic, she let me use her cabin boy to take the food up. He proved to be every bit as nimble as the man I'd watched climbing the riggings earlier.

When everything was arranged to my satisfaction, the hard work began. None of my plans would work if she refused to come with me in the first place. This was where the good captain had been a little more uncertain. As she rightly pointed out, the romantic evening would only work if Gwen was willing to take a chance. That was when she'd left me on my own, slapping me on the back, and heading back to work.

After running through at least a dozen scenarios, I gave up and went to find Gwen. When I finally found her, she was relaxing below deck with her wolves. No one else was around, which suited my needs.

I was sure the guys were hanging out with the other crewmembers, learning, a variety of useful and-or dangerous skills. I cleared my throat at the doorway, and she looked up.

We locked eyes for a moment, but it wasn't an easy experience like it had always been before. We looked away at the same time, and I almost lost my nerve until I recalled what Captain Baeley told me.

I was a Librarian. A keeper of knowledge, an adventurer, explorer, and warrior. I was not willing to give up without a fight. I cleared my throat again, earning a perplexed frown. At least she was paying attention now, so I dove right in.

"Can you come with me for a minute? There's something I'd like to show you."

To my surprised ears, my voice sounded calm and

collected, betraying none of my inner turmoil. I wondered what she saw as she searched my face. I wasn't sure she'd found the answer she was looking for but was relieved when she finally nodded.

"Okay. Can I bring the wolves?"

I looked at Swift, who almost seemed to be smiling. I felt strangely as though he was wishing me good luck. But surely, that was silly.

"*Err*, umm, you could... But I don't think they'll like where we're going. Perhaps leave them here for now?"

I had nothing against the wolves, but I was certain they wouldn't enjoy the crow's nest. I was also selfish enough to want her all to myself without a furry buffer. I didn't want her using them as a barrier between us. This was our chance to either make up or move on, depending how everything went. Oh, how I prayed we made up.

She said a quick goodbye to the wolves and followed silently behind me as I climbed the stairs onto the deck. She didn't speak until we got to the pole of the crow's nest, where I gestured for her to go first up the rope stairs on the mast.

"Are you serious?" The wide-eyed look of fear she gave me wasn't a good start, but I pressed on.

"Captain Baeley showed me the crow's nest earlier. I thought maybe you'd enjoy it, since you live in a treehouse and all."

She looked dubious, but to my great relief, she took a deep breath and began to climb. I'd hoped to help her up at the top, but if she was scared enough of heights to lose her balance, I'd be able to help. It also ensured she didn't change her mind without me knowing halfway up.

I reached the crow's nest a second behind her, holding my breath while I waited for her reaction. To my relief, it wasn't anger. Her beautiful face held the same mixture of confusion and hope I was feeling inside, and it gave me the courage I needed.

"I've been trying to find an opportunity to talk with you, ever since you told me how you felt."

She flushed and looked away as if unable to meet my eyes.

I stepped closer, needing to reassure her I hadn't found her touch abhorrent. I gently took her chin in my hand and steered her face back to mine, giving her plenty of room to pull away.

Her breathing sped up, as though she couldn't get enough air. I stepped closer, stopping just before our bodies were touching. Heat engulfed me, and I felt my face burn, starting at my throat, then traveling all the way to the tip of my ears. Words were now completely gone from my mind.

I took one more step, and we were touching.

Chest to chest, belly to belly.

My arms went around her the same instant hers came around me.

I fell into summertime.

The kiss stretched out, doing things to my soul I never expected to feel. The warmth had been unexpected, but as it blossomed into a raging fire, it sent shivers over my body. Now I was the one unable to catch my breath, enraptured by the magic spell she was weaving over every inch of my being.

The kiss deepened. Her heart thudded against mine, her raspy breathing brushed my face. Together, we sank to our knees. For all its intensity, the kiss was gentle, testing. Soft lips questing, searching for answers, and opening to let them in.

Entangled in each other, it wasn't until I found myself on the floor with the smell of grapes and bread in my nose reality slowly returned.

I pulled back reluctantly, gasping, heart fluttering as I looked into her eyes for several breathless moments. What had I done?

Her cheeks flushed, her hair beautifully askew, I watched nervously as she swallowed. It wasn't until a crooked smile spread over her face, I allowed myself to hope.

She rolled onto her back and stretched her arms all the way

to the side. "Now, that is what I call an apology." She burst into laughter, staring up at the clouds scuttling by in the rapidly darkening sky.

I rolled onto my elbow to watch her, resting my face on my hand. Her chest rose slower now, and I waited until she looked at me again.

"I meant to actually apologize." I dropped my hand flat against the wood, shaking my head as I searched for words. "Don't misunderstand, the kiss was absolutely amazing, but it wasn't supposed to be my apology. I wasn't even sure you'd come up here with me, after how you've been avoiding me since I screwed up. I meant to apologize with words, to show you how much you mean to me. See, I even packed a picnic."

I gestured at the food, some of which had been knocked aside during our embrace.

She rolled her head to the side to gaze at me, smiling the way she used to, her eyes crinkling at the corners the way I loved.

"True, but I'm different from you. I'm sure your apology would've been amazing, but this," she gestured at the food as she looked at me. "I'm not complex the way you are. Words aren't the most important things. Maybe because my best friends are wolves, emotions and actions speak loudest to me. You could've apologized until the sun came up tomorrow and I might not have believed you. But when you came to me, crowded me," her eyelashes fluttered, giving her eyes a hooded, mysterious look as her gaze warmed me, "the way you kissed me. All of that shows me how you feel more than a simple verbal apology ever could."

I exhaled and slid closer, tucking my head into her shoulder. Her arm wrapped around me easily, like I was meant to be there. Joy filled me as we lay silently for a few minutes. I enjoyed feeling her heartbeat, the soft rise and fall of her chest beside me. The heat of attraction was there, but tucked away now, to be acted upon later. I didn't want to rush anything, for her or myself.

It was all so new.

"I've never felt like this for anyone." I turned my head slightly, meeting her eyes.

She pressed a kiss to my forehead. "I know now. I'm sorry I overreacted. It was hard to tell you how I felt ... well, you know. Words aren't my strong suit. Neither are social interactions with anyone other than my wolves. I've had a crush on you for a long time, but I'd always thought it was a silly fancy. Me, a wolf-walker basically shunned by all Elven kind, and you, the gorgeous, smart scholar from the castle. What chance did I have? I had no reason to think you returned my affection and planned never to tell you. When you came to me with the request to help you on a crazy quest to stop Dag'draath and the complete devastation of our world, how could I say no?"

She shrugged, her words matter of fact and heartbreaking in their raw honesty.

I allowed myself to caress her cheek as I looked into her marvelous eyes.

"I had no idea. When you told me in the tavern, I wasn't trying to reject you, I'd just never considered it. Not the part where you had feelings for me, when you're the one who's amazing, certainly not my own feelings. As Will has so helpfully pointed out more than once since you ran off, I'm not exactly good with social interactions either."

She pressed her chin into my hand, and I marveled at the softness of her skin.

"Don't cut yourself down," she admonished softly, pressing a kiss into my palm, and placing it on her heart. "You've been nothing but inspiring this whole trip. I was worried about your abilities to travel, to be perfectly honest, but every step of our trip you've shown me you are so much more than a mere scholar.

"I've watched you fight, pick up new skills like fire building, hunting, and constructing a shelter. Maybe not with ease, exactly," she teased, her eyes twinkling, "but with effort and hard work which have impressed me. As for social interactions, well, pot calling the kettle black. Maybe if I'd been better at expressing my emotions and words, I wouldn't have run off looking for a fight at the merest hint of rejection."

"We were both to blame for our miscommunication. Can you promise to let me know if I ever do something that upsets you? I never want to hurt you. You're my best friend." I blushed, placing the tip of my tongue in my cheek as I tried to think what I was supposed to call her now, to call this unexpected fire.

Her eyes followed my gesture, darkening, and I felt an answering pulse of heat low in my belly. As though caught in a web she'd cast, my lips sought hers again.

I wasn't sure how long we'd spent wrapped up together, only that every inch of my body felt alive in a way it had never felt before. I was filled with energy. In the moment, I could do anything. I could climb every mountain, fight every ur'gel I came across. Being with her as a friend, companion, and now as a lover filled me with a power I'd never expected to feel, and never wanted to let go of.

When we reluctantly pulled apart later, smoothing back each other's hair, placing soft kisses and tender touches on arms and faces, when my heartbeat had finally settled to more normal rhythms, she answered a question I hadn't had a chance to ask before I'd become distracted.

"It may be far too soon to call it this, but I want you to know I consider you to be more than a friend or lover. From the moment I met you, your being sang to my soul. I may not be good with my words, but one thing I do know is the shape of someone on the inside. I know I haven't told you much about my dreams, but sometimes, I see things." She hesitated, her eyes wide with anxiety and I leaned closer, taking her hand, and giving it a soft squeeze of encouragement.

She exhaled shakily before continuing. "I've seen us together there, in my dreams. I felt the rightness. But it's more than I can express."

I understood what she was trying to say, even though it didn't make sense. "We're meant to be together."

A smile crept across her face. "Yes. I see a lot of terrible things, and lately they've been getting worse, but the one thing always buoying me and giving me hope is what I see for us. It might sound strange, especially because we didn't know each other very well prior to our journey, but I think you're my soulmate."

A rush of joy filled me, brighter and more glorious even than what her touch had stirred. "I was looking for a word for this. Soulmate." Peace followed on the heels of the joy.

"My friend, partner, soulmate."

CHAPTER 11

After our crow's nest date, things returned to normal between us. Well, not normal—better. It was the happiest I'd ever been. When we returned to the bunk room much later, we wished each other good night at the door, sharing one last kiss before reluctantly parting and entering. We still had to share the bunk room with the guys, and neither of us was ready to take our relationship further. Not yet, at least.

It was late, but neither of them was asleep when we walked in. The look on their faces made it clear they knew we'd quite literally kissed and made up, but they didn't question us, for which I'd been grateful. I wasn't ready to talk about it with anyone yet. With all the emotional turmoil of the past few days resolved, I had the best sleep of my life.

When I jolted awake by almost falling out of my birth at the sudden turbulence, I was immediately alert. It was a particularly rude awakening, as I'd been dreaming about my date and reliving the moment we'd made up. It took a moment to remember where I was as I looked around, but once I was reoriented, I thought It sounded like the roof was caving in. Inside the bunk room, everything appeared normal, except all our belongings were on the floor, as was Sel. Apparently, the same thud which had woken me had thrown him completely out of bed.

"What's going on?" Gwen looked around fearfully through sleepy eyes.

It was easy to see she still hadn't completely gotten over her fear of flying. The turbulence restored the same pinched, white face she'd worn the first time we'd boarded. The wolves were awake as well and moving restlessly on the floor beside her.

It appeared we'd all been woken in the same way. The only one who appeared unperturbed was Will, although at the next large jolt, even he had a tough time hiding his surprise.

I got off my bunk, wobbling against the ongoing lurching of the ship around and beneath me, and carefully made my way to the door. When I pulled it open, the wind almost took my breath away. I immediately changed direction and struggled against the gale force wind outside to push it shut. I turned to rest my back against it, breathing hard from the effort as I looked at the others.

"It's super windy out there. I think we're flying through a storm."

Will shook his head, getting off his bed and coming toward me in a strange crab-like and similarly cautious fashion. "No, this is the reason Captain Baeley didn't want to take us all the way to the Northwestern Lands. I know she told us the ship won't work because of the magic, but she *may* have left out the part about the winds."

I looked at him, aghast, vaguely hearing Sel's groans in the background as he got off the floor. "Winds? What winds? I didn't read about them, and she never mentioned anything."

I narrowed my eyes as I thought back over what I'd read about the land we were heading to. Nope, nothing about winds.

"She told me the other day. I'm not sure where you were." He gave me a look, slyly moving his gaze to Gwen, smirking, then returning to the conversation. "Which is neither here nor there. Apparently, the last mountain range before the Dragon Dominion ends and the Northwestern Lands begins is horrible. No one goes there. Any ship that tries is wrecked or has pieces blown clear off. Basically, it's not something any sane captain is willing to attempt."

He gave me a pointed look, raising his eyebrows. "The only reason Captain Baeley took us this far is because she believes in the mission of a Librarian. You must have made quite an impression on her, Princess. I don't think any other pilot would've taken us even this far."

Had I somehow convinced her to do something dangerous in ways I hadn't anticipated? I remembered the story about the other airship crash she'd told us about and shuddered. I hadn't thought I was doing anything wrong, but with the ship lurching in loud and increasingly horrible ways, my gut clenched with a combination of guilt and fear.

"What should we do?"

"I think we should stay here, out of the way until we hear otherwise. We don't want to get in the way of people doing the work to keep us alive, or chance being blown overboard by a rogue gust."

"Sounds like a wise plan to me," Gwen agreed quickly. "Until further notice, I'm going to spend all my time here, in the bunk room. Call me if you need anything." Her words were glib, but her wide eyes gave her away.

I pressed my lips together as I debated my options. On the one hand, staying below deck sounded like a good idea. But on the other, I needed to know what was happening above deck. I made up my mind. Turning to Will, I knew what I was going to say wasn't going to go over well.

"I want to find her. I need to ask what's going to happen next, but I promise I'll come right back." I bit the inside of my cheek as I waited for their response. As I'd expected, I didn't have to wait long.

"Are you crazy?" He looked at me as if I had sprouted a second head. "No offense, but you aren't exactly what I'd consider the nimblest of people. Of all of us, you're the one I most worry would get blown overboard."

"Thanks for the vote of confidence."

I did my best to keep my voice even and patient, although I had a sudden intense longing to punch him for the way he was looking down his nose at me.

"Either way, in order to know where to head after we land, I need a better sense of the terrain where we are now. If the winds are as bad as you say, I imagine she's going to want to land at the bottom of the mountain as soon as possible. "

His eyebrows dropped. "True, okay, fine. But I'm coming with you if you're going. Is there a rope in here?"

We all looked, but it was Sel, who found it, thanks to his position on the floor a moment earlier, pulled out a large spool of heavy rope underneath the bunk he'd been sleeping in.

"Perfect. Rhin come here. I'm going to tie it around your waist and attach you to me the same way."

I wrinkled my nose, looking dubiously from him to the rope and back.

He rolled his eyes. "Don't worry, I'll give you plenty of lead. At least this way if one of us gets blown over, the other should be able to pull the castaway back. It's as much for my protection as yours," he assured me, although I could tell from his eyes, he was worried about me.

It was interesting how the longer I spent with him, how his hidden qualities became more apparent. It did help explain how someone as cocky as Will could have a friend as studious as Jarid. The thought crossed my mind that maybe he put out his own version of a façade for society, the same way I did.

Realizing he was waiting for a reply, I shook my head and agreed. "Okay, fine. But be quick. I have a feeling the good captain is going to be busy. The sooner we get out of her way, the happier she'll be."

. . .

I PUT my thumb between the rope and my waist, tugging on it slightly. It was tight, but I could still breathe easily, which was good I guessed. It wasn't the most comfortable situation, but the logic of using the rope soothed me as we walked, or should I say fought, our way up the stairs above deck.

Keeping my eyes narrowed to keep the howling wind from drying them out, I could barely see the deckhands running from side to side battening down the hatches. Everything which had been loose was gone. I wasn't sure if it was because they'd put it away, or if it had been sent overboard. Either way, this was as good a time as any.

Praying no unexpected projectiles hit me, I allowed Will to go first. I followed in his wake, thankful his larger frame blocked some of the wind, although I was still able to feel its cold bite. I caught glimpses of desert between the jagged mountains, and knew we were just on the other side. It wasn't a warm desert like I'd thought, at least, the mountainside wasn't.

Spotting Captain Baeley at the stern, he struggled to reach her.

I followed as closely as possible, occasionally getting blown back and fighting the wind to catch up.

When she saw us approaching, she shook her head. She looked furious.

I imagined I'd be irritated too if I oversaw everyone aboard a ship and some silly travelers thought it was a good idea to get in the way of nature.

"Where are we?" His question was instantly stolen by the wind.

Her words were faint but audible against the din as she called back. "The last mountain range. We're going to head straight down the side and try to land before the ship breaks apart. Get below deck now! That's an order!"

I peeked from behind his back, grimacing. "I just wanted to know where we were. I need to know which direction to head when we land."

"You'll do what I tell you. This is non-negotiable. Below deck now. We can deal with directions if we don't die."

I nodded meekly, giving her my best salute, and tugged on Will's shoulder before doing exactly as ordered and heading below deck. The ominous sound of wood creaking, and possibly even breaking off, supported her words and I saw no reason to argue.

We were hardly through the doors when Gwen launched herself at me.

"Hey," I said softly, returning her hug, "everything's fine." I'd used my most reassuring voice, but I could tell she didn't believe me.

She pulled back, her eyes large and worried. "What's it like up there?"

A faint tremble in her voice made her sound younger. It was odd seeing her afraid, so I smiled, trying to sound confident. I kept her hand in mine as I moved into the room, pulling her down to sit with me on a bunk. The sound of the wood groaning and wind battering at the side of the ship made it necessary to speak louder.

"Pretty much what it sounds like. The winds are extremely fierce. Captain Baeley and the crew are working hard to land. We're at our destination, I guess." I gave her a tight smile, patting her hand. "She's going to try and land at the base of the mountain. This is where we get off. Nothing she can do about it. The winds are too strong for any ship to survive the other side so it's as far as we can travel with her."

She took a few deep breaths. "So, we should be ready to leave?"

"We may as well be. Make sure all your stuff is packed so when we land, we can go."

Will and I exchanged a look as they went to their bunks to

pack their belongings. We both knew I'd downplayed the severity of what was going on above-deck, but it wouldn't do them any good to worry. At least packing kept us busy for a while, with the additional bonus of Will tossing me Jarid's copy of the two-way book, which I added to my satchel for easy access.

It was almost an hour later when a louder, more violent thump almost threw us across the room. My heart skipped, then I realized we weren't moving. I looked at my friends with a faint smile.

"I think that means we've landed." I turned to Will. "Do you think it's safe to go up and look around?"

Will cocked his head, listening. An eerie silence had replaced the wind which had been howling only a moment earlier and I hoped the change meant we were out of danger.

"Sure. We may as well all go."

I watched him bite the inside of his cheek. I'd never seen him look uncertain before now. He was probably remembering how she'd told us to get below and stay there.

I considered staying where we were until she came to get us, looking toward the door uncertainly.

No one moved.

When I decided to act, though, Will strode to the door a moment before I got up.

He was halfway there when it flew open.

Captain Baeley stood in the doorway, looking tired but pleased. "We did it. We landed and should be in good enough shape to take off again safely. If you come up, I'll show you which direction you need to travel to get to your coordinates.

Gwen's faced relaxed with relief, and she leaned over to communicate with the wolves. The guys followed the captain out the door, but I waited for Gwen to pick her items up.

We walked up the stairs, hand in hand, and I had the feeling we'd waged and won a war against nature itself.

Once above deck, I could see there had been some damage

to the ship, but the way the crew were attending to it made me hopeful it was minor, and they'd be able to repair it and take off shortly. I hated knowing I'd put her into this situation. I'd had no idea about the severity of the winds.

When we reached the gangplank, I turned and looked awkwardly at my feet, then at her. She appeared smooth and unruffled again, but I knew it had been a hard trip, and all because of me.

"I wanted to say thank you. You've done so much for us, for me, I just don't have the words to tell you how much I appreciate everything."

She waved her hand, brushing my gratitude aside. "It was nothing. Just keep me in mind for your next adventure, Princess. I always love traveling with a Librarian. You never know what's gonna happen next."

The others added their thanks, and as we turned to leave, I caught Sel casting regretful, longing looks back at the ship. I had a feeling once our adventures were over, if we survived them of course, I'd offer him his freedom and nudge him toward considering the life of an air captain. It seemed like something he'd be good at.

We reached the bottom and turned as the airship lifted off. Exhaling in relief the ship was able to fly, I waved one last goodbye.

Captain Baeley waved back then suddenly, her face drained of color and her eyes widened. When a few nearby crew members assumed similar expressions, I knew our next adventure had begun, whether I wanted it to or not.

I turned to see what they had seen and looked straight at the terrifying shapes of the Oubliee.

I'd read about them, of course, but never expected or hoped to see them. The pictures hadn't done them justice. Although they were apparently human beneath their attire, they seemed somehow more terrifying than any I'd ever seen.

They were desert nomads, the only group known to still live in the deserts of the Northwestern Lands.

Their faces were completely obscured by the brown, shapeless swaths of fabric they wore, but they were clearly not happy we were there. Every figure held a vicious looking weapon, which they pointed toward us menacingly.

Based on the gestures the one in the front was making with a long-pointed spear, they appeared to be inviting us to go with them.

CHAPTER 12

Rough hands gripped my wrists, binding them with a thick, uncomfortable rope like the one Will had tied around my waist earlier. Had it only been a few hours ago? They weren't as careful as he'd been, and my wrists already burned from the restriction. Once we were bound together, they'd firmly led us out of the mountain pass.

So far, they hadn't been abusive, which I was grateful for. We didn't put up a fight, because even with the wolves we were overwhelmingly outnumbered. To my surprise, they'd seemed almost excited when they'd seen the animals.

The Oubliee didn't speak a language I could understand, but their quick gestures and the way they'd looked at the wolves and at each other, allowing them to walk unrestrained alongside Gwen indicated to me they held them in higher esteem than us.

I realized then I hadn't seen any of our abductors speak. In fact, I wasn't even sure they had mouths. Each of them wore huge swathes of fabric and were wrapped head to toe everywhere but a narrow slit allowing their uniformly dark eyes to see.

. . .

I WASN'T sure how many of the nomads there were. Some walked behind us, to ensure we didn't escape, I assumed, but I estimated there were at least fifty of them. After several silent minutes where we hadn't been hit or otherwise injured or spoken to, I tried to speak to the captor I assumed was the leader.

"Please, we are looking for something. We were only passing through, but our ship had to land here unexpectedly. We didn't mean to trespass and if you set us free, we'll leave, I promise."

Either they didn't speak our language, or they were under instructions to take us regardless. Either way, he didn't reply. During the entire abduction, not a single one of the group spoke to us as they led us down a path from the mountain side into the heart of the desert itself.

"Please," I begged, looking at the captor in front of me. "If you take us to your leader, I can explain. We mean no harm. We aren't dangerous."

I may as well have been speaking old Elvish for the reaction I got. Other than a slight narrowing of his dark brown eyes, the Oubliee pushing me along didn't respond at all. Maybe they didn't understand me?

If it hadn't been for what I'd read about them, I would question their humanity more than I already was. It didn't take long until I understood why they were covered the way they were as we walked into the desert.

The force of the wind had diminished at our landing, but it became stronger as we left the relative shelter of the mountains and replaced it with the sand of the desert. While individually each grain was tiny, when whipped up by the winds we were walking through, the sand cut and hurt.

I found myself trying in vain to cover more of my face with my hair and clothing but hampered as I was by the ropes on my wrists, nothing I did seemed to help. It still found its way in through the cracks between my tunic and neck, stinging my face as the wind blew my hair into my eyes.

I struggled to keep up, knowing if I faltered, my captors would surely drag me instead. Glimpses of my friends told me they were being subjected to the same treatment. Not abused, exactly, but neither were any of us shown any consideration. Except the wolves, who were occasionally slipped treats, which I found unusual.

To my surprise, even though Gwen had been tied up the same way I'd been, the wolves hadn't attacked our captors. They looked worried, but also resigned, as if they knew something we didn't.

Perhaps the fact the Oubliee weren't speaking to us meant they could communicate another way.

All I knew was the wolves were following without being tied or maltreated. Perhaps the Oubliee weren't completely bad, although I may have been fooling myself.

My body was exhausted by the time I finally caught a glimpse of civilization. It seemed to be trading town surrounded by a large earthen wall. The wall appeared to be several stories high, and as I squinted against the wind still whipping the painful sand around, I could see Oubliee on the walls.

They nodded at our captors, relaxing their hold on the spears they held prominently in front of them. A loud grating sound rumbled, and a large wooden door slammed onto the ground, giving passage through the wall into the town.

The moment we were inside, a thump made me start. I looked over my shoulder to see the door had closed behind me. One improvement I immediately appreciated was the moment the door shut, sand stopped biting my face. To my surprise, my captor removed a layer of the material from his face. Once the covering was gone, I was relieved to see a normal, dark-skinned human had been beneath the material all along.

During our forced march, I'd almost begun to believe they

had no mouths or other human features except for eyes. I had started to create disturbing images of smooth faced demons to fill in the mystery, so I was relieved to find it was just a figment of my imagination.

They may have been human, but our captors still pushed and dragged us through town toward an undisclosed location like they thought we were property. It was hard to examine my surroundings in detail due to the speed they shoved us along, but the houses I could see as we passed were made of a smooth, sand-colored material.

Most appeared barely large enough for one room except for a few taller buildings, which looked like several of the smaller ones stuck together into what I assumed were multi-family dwellings. Fabric hung on lines between the taller buildings and in the alleys between the smaller ones, but little in the way of vegetation broke up the sandy colors of the town.

My captor abruptly stopped, and I stumbled and fell. I quickly righted myself on shaky legs as my captor glared at me. Once I was standing again, he turned to the front. I followed his gaze.

We had stopped in front of one of the larger buildings, but this was different than the ones on the outskirts. It was lighter colored and thicker, more solidly built. Perhaps it was the bars on the windows of the lower level which gave me the impression of sturdiness.

I swallowed hard, noticing they were speaking to each other. I glanced at the bars, certain of what they meant for us.

Almost immediately, we were manhandled into a small extension of the main building. It jutted off the side and didn't require entrance through the main door. Instead, it appeared to be an animal pen. It was open to the air on the sides but fenced in with metal and shared its roof with the main building.

I hoped it was a temporary holding place, otherwise our captors weren't concerned with keeping hostages alive for more than a few days. I knew myself well enough to know I wouldn't last long under these conditions, even if it was warm enough not to freeze to death.

The comforting weight of my bag bouncing lightly against my side brought me back. We'd been searched before they'd tied us up, but after they'd removed my knife, they'd taken one look at the books and dirty clothes and roughly shoved it back at me.

Apparently, they weren't impressed. But it did give me options I wouldn't have otherwise had. While it wasn't a weapon, I still had the book to communicate with Jarid.

I didn't know what he'd be able to do for us here though, as he could hardly send help. I didn't know where we were, and even if I did, help wouldn't arrive in time if the Oubliee planned to harm us.

Our kidnappers dispersed once we were safely installed in the outdoor cage, leaving only one of the younger men to stand guard at the door. It was just the four of us in this prison, and I looked at them. Gwen's face was stormy, anger nearly radiating from her face.

The guys, on the other hand, looked more scuffed up. Will had a bruise on one cheek and his face was dirty, while Sel had a small cut above his lip. I hadn't noticed a difference when we'd been tied up, but now suspected they'd treated us more gently because we were women.

Gwen's eyes met mine and saw relief fill her face as she looked me over and saw I was unharmed as well. Once satisfied all my friends were relatively intact, I narrowed my gaze, turning in toward our prison to assess the situation.

I stayed silent, unsure if our guard spoke our language. If he did, it was possible any conversation we had could be used against us. I was still holding out hope we'd have a chance to speak to an authority of some sort. Maybe they'd let us continue our search but based on their taciturn and brusque attitude so far, my naïve hope was quickly fading.

"Hey, over here."

A soft female voice seemed to float to me from somewhere near the back of the cage. I turned my head swiftly, squinting at the corner beside the thick stone wall which made up the back of our cage and the metal cage at the side where the voice had sounded from. At first, it looked like an empty space with wooden barrels leaning haphazardly on top of each other.

Then I saw her.

She was crouched behind the barrels, with only her head peeking between the wall and the top of one of the bars. She appeared human but wasn't anyone I'd seen before. My eyebrows went up and I looked to see if the others had seen her. I found them as startled by the unexpected presence of the woman as I'd been, watching her with matching silent, wide-eyed expressions.

Once the initial surprise wore off, Will inclined his head, flashing a cocky smile which made me feel strangely better under the circumstances. If he could still try to be annoying, somehow, it made me feel things weren't all too bad.

He sidled over to the section of the wall where the woman was hiding, making sure to move slow enough for his movements to seem unplanned. When he reached the far corner, he stretched, sat on the floor, and leaned back on the barrels, bringing his knees up and wrapping his arms around them, as though he'd found a place to have a nap.

I marveled at how subtle he could be. With his head resting on his knees and turned slightly toward the corner where the woman hid, he almost did appear to be sleeping. It was only when you looked directly at him from closer was it possible to see his eyes fixed firmly on an object to his right.

I shifted closer to Gwen, keeping an eye on the guard as I arranged myself next to her to form a barrier. It wasn't much, but he'd have to look past, or over us, to see what Will was doing. Sel, string bean he was, moved closer to the guard to keep an eye and serve as a lookout. All of this was completed silently in seconds.

The woman spoke again. "My name is Nyalla." Her voice was so low it was barely audible, even though I was only a few feet away. "I want to help you escape. If you trust me, I will get you out of here."

"What are they planning to do with us? Why did they take us?"

He asked exactly what I wanted to know, and I strained my ears to hear her reply.

"They are scavengers. I'm guessing you were in the wrong place, but it is how they work. Most likely they've already stripped everything of value from wherever you came from. The men who left you here are going to find out their orders. They work for someone else of course and will go on long trips for supplies. Sometimes they find objects, sometimes they bring home slaves. Once they get their orders, they'll come back for you. They'll probably take you to the temple, so be ready. I'll try to break you out."

"Why do you want to help us?" He spoke louder.

I winced, looking at the guard. Luckily, he either hadn't heard or didn't care if his prisoners were talking.

There was a long pause before the woman answered. "Because I–"

I gasped as the woman was yanked to her feet. I saw the face of the man who'd overseen pushing me along the path and realized he must be the leader of the kidnappers.

He looked irritated as he glared at the woman. He leaned closer to her until his face was almost touching and proceeded to yell at her.

I didn't understand what he was saying, but it wasn't hard to tell she wasn't supposed to be there.

She cowered in his grip and the change in her position allowed me to get a better look at our would-be rescuer. She was strikingly beautiful, with long dark hair and tanned complexion like the other humans we'd seen here, but she had a presence about her the others hadn't.

I wasn't sure if it was merely because she was so beautiful, or if it was something more than her looks, I was sensing.

Even as she trembled in the larger man's grip, something in her bearing made her seem less afraid than I would expect from someone in her situation.

The man stopped screaming, but was now looking at her with his nose in the air and his lip wrinkled, as if she was something disgusting he'd stepped in. It was odd but interesting, especially because she was so pretty.

Then he dropped her, letting her go as though she wasn't worth his time, or he was worried he would catch something.

She fell onto her backside, making angry hand gestures at him as she got up. She spit emphatically at the ground before stalking off.

I couldn't help feeling our chance at escape had just left angry and my spirits sank, especially when the man walked around to the front of the cage and spoke with the guard on duty.

I couldn't make out what the discussion was about, but the young guard nodded before unlocking the door and handing the key to the larger man.

The larger man entered, stopping a few feet inside and leaving the door open behind him. Planting his feet shoulder-width apart, he crossed his arms. If he hadn't been intimidating before, he certainly was now. His tense stance made his arms look immense, as if his sleeves were struggling to contain his muscles and on the verge of losing.

His face was etched in hard lines of disapproval as he narrowed ice-cold brown eyes at us. I wasn't sure if his sour look was left over from his conversation with Nyalla or due to our presence.

"You will now come with me."

This time, I could understand him. The lack of conversation had been intentional, not a function of a lack of mouths as

I'd convinced myself initially, or a lack of shared language, which I'd hoped for.

They had been ignoring us all this time.

Nice.

I added arrogant to the list of characteristics for this man.

When no one moved, his eyes hardened further, if possible. "Now!"

As he barked the command, his arms moved to his sides. When I saw his hands ball into fists beside his massive thighs, I jumped up.

He didn't look like the kind of man who would ask again.

I was relieved when the others sprang up as well. I had no idea what he wanted from us but doing what he wanted would help to keep things as calm as possible until I'd had a chance to size the situation up.

"You will come with me. We shall go see the Sovran."

I glanced at Gwen, seeing the same confused look on her face I was sure I was wearing. I turned to the man, but bit back the question at the closed, unyielding look on his face.

Once he was content we were listening to his instructions, he gestured for us to follow. Surprisingly, he didn't bother tying us up again. This single omission alone led me to assume they didn't think of us as a threat, which was both insulting and a little worrisome. I was so grateful they'd removed the ropes after throwing us in the cage I wasn't about to give them a reason to assume differently though, at least, not yet.

I was directly behind the larger man, noting the same young man who'd been our guard was bringing up the rear. They might not feel we were dangerous, but they weren't foolish enough to think we wouldn't walk off given a chance. The fact they were leading us to Suun knew where in such a fashion only reinforced my sense they were confident of quelling a four-against-two fight and didn't feel the need to make an effort to even the odds, was in fact, quite sobering.

Then again, they possibly had never heard the phrase

'looks could be deceiving.' I knew they were keeping a closer eye on Will than Gwen or me, as he was the strongest in appearance. But I'd seen her fight, and I wasn't sure who'd come out ahead if they ever fought in earnest.

Sel had proven himself wiry and resourceful more than once, and after being in the Library, I seemed to have picked up enough fighting ability to single-handedly demolish the slaver who'd been after the wolves. Facts I wasn't going to share but may use to my advantage after we found out where they were taking us and why. Hopefully, it was to someone who'd tell us why the Oubliee had taken us in the first place.

As we walked, I hoped the others were of the same mindset as I was. I didn't risk talking or looking back. We passed several houses, and I couldn't help but feeling curious about the town itself. We may be prisoners, but the place we'd been brought to functioned the same as every other village from what I could see.

Animals kept in small backyards in pens, children darted in and out of the streets, playing together with shrieks and laughter.

Women chatted between houses as they worked on mending, weaving, or hanged laundry to dry.

Men went about their days carrying loads, running stores, chatting in the streets, or on benches with other men. Apart from the village area being entirely covered by sand and sand-colored buildings, we could have been in one of the Low Forest settlements.

At least, until the leader stopped moving.

I stared, my eyes widening as they traveled all the way to the top of the edifice in front of me. I'd seen some buildings which were taller when we'd arrived, but none were anywhere as impressive as this one. It was clearly a building of importance.

Approximately three stories tall, it was intricately carved on every surface, save for those acting as a blank space between pictures. It was made of the same sandstone, but the carvings and elegant latticework on immense columns framing the front of the building made the plain rock seem to shimmer in the desert sun. Windows were lined with busts of both people and mythological animals, sparkling with a clear, wavering material I didn't recognize in the center.

The leader turned, nodded once to the guard in the back and gestured for us to follow before he turned and entered. I followed tentatively, my footsteps echoing as they stepped lightly on the hard-stone floor.

The foyer was enormous, its ceiling stretching almost the height of the building outside. Each level had a staircase I could see which opened into the foyer. Windows provided light and there were even a few lush green trees. I'd never seen trees like those before. They looked like they could be the remnants of the abundant tropical growth the books I'd read had mentioned.

I glanced at Gwen whose eyes were wide as she looked around.

"Wow." She mouthed.

I nodded in agreement, but we didn't have time to stop and marvel as we were escorted to a set of dark wood doors with large bronze handles.

The leader paused a moment to allow the two servants who'd been standing beside the door to grab a handle each and pull them open before walking straight in ... to the middle of a royal court.

Supplicants lined the floor along a center aisle. A man was kneeling with his head on the floor at the base of an ornately decorated chair where a woman sat, one ankle crossed over her knee, her head held regally as she watched him. She appeared to be listening as he pleaded with her for something. Her expression gave nothing away, and her eyes remained hooded.

I was beginning to think every woman in this town was so beautiful they turned heads. The woman who'd offered to break us out had been striking, but this woman was doubly so. Although arguably not as attractive, there was something about her appearance I found even more arresting.

She had a strong, curved nose, like a bird of prey. Large, deep set eyes, a startling ice- blue peered at the man on the floor beneath eyelids painted a brilliant indigo. Her hair was tucked up beneath an ornate head wrapping.

It was similar in style to those of the men who'd captured us, but far more luxurious in fabric and draping. Her clothing appeared to provide the same protection from the desert sands as the men's plainer attire, but hers was a blinding bright white instead of the drab brown they'd worn.

She was undoubtably the leader the men had left us earlier to speak with. When she noticed us enter, she stood. She made a slashing movement with her hand and the room fell silent.

"My name is Sovran Jaydra Din Hariri. What in the name of Hatthi are you doing in my desert?

CHAPTER 13

The fierce woman before us exuded power.

I didn't know if it was her personality or magic, but I felt it radiating from every pore. It made me, the daughter of a noble family, feel as if I was supposed to bow down in her presence.

Instead, I took a deep breath and approached her slowly, walking down the aisle. I thought for sure I'd be held back or stopped by the leader of the scavengers, but he'd stepped aside as soon as the sovran had stood.

Apparently, even though we were prisoners, we could speak for ourselves. Not necessarily a boon, as I'd watched travelers to the Cliffs plead their case to my father and make their situation worse. Especially ones who were unfamiliar with our local customs. Now, I was in the same situation and I swallowed, hard.

Glancing at the others, I could see their worried expressions as they waited for me to speak. They didn't stop me, and I knew they were hoping my 'princess' title would help us now. Even though I wasn't the best at reading others, I was the most practiced with court etiquette. Praying manners here weren't so different from home, I approached the throne.

When I was almost to the kneeling man, I bowed deeply and crossed my right arm over my chest. Waiting at the most deferential angle, I didn't move until the sovran spoke.

"Stand up." She sounded reluctantly amused as well as impatient, so I rose immediately.

Tilting my head to the side, I acknowledged the honor of receiving her attention. "Thank you, it is an honor to meet you, Sovran. We were attempting to travel to the Northwestern Lands when we had a rough landing. I'm sure you are aware the winds are fierce over the last mountain range of the Dragon Dominion. Our airship had just landed when we were greeted by your men."

I deliberately kept my voice even, holding back my urge to demand restitution. Technically, we hadn't been in the desert lands yet, which meant we weren't trespassing. But I didn't want to risk angering her before I had a chance to ask for help.

"Were you?" Jaydra practically purred the words, the softness giving them a dangerous edge.

I knew I'd been wise not to add any censure to my tone, but it was clear I'd pushed my luck far enough with my greeting alone. From the look on her face, it seemed as if she was a leader who felt everything her people touched belonged to them, and by extension, to her. Perhaps this was why the strange woman, Nyalla, had tried to rescue us.

"Yes, we were unaware we were on your property. We beg forgiveness for our breach in manners. We are merely lost travelers, searching for an item we hope will bring light to the darkness crossing the land. The moment we find it, we will depart without delay."

I was taking a calculated risk. Although most humans, elves, and other creatures not born of darkness supported Dag'draath remaining in prison, I knew not everyone did.

There were those in all species who felt allowing him out would be the proper thing to do and provide a fitting end to a battle some felt ended unfairly through trickery by Suun.

I had no way to know which side the Oubliee fell on, but I was hoping our mission would pique her interest at least enough to help us.

"*You* are searching for an item? What type of item? And what makes you think your trip is either necessary or worthwhile?" She crossed her arms, looking down her nose at me with one perfectly arched eyebrow raised.

I took a deep breath, working to control my temper. It was a valid question, even if it did make me feel as irritated as when Kramson or Luban judged me at the Library. Who *was* I to speak to her? I stood tall and looked at her proudly.

"I am a Librarian from Abrecem Secer. I am on a mission for the Library and for the greater good of Lynia to find an item to allow me to stop the oncoming war before anyone else is lost to a massacre. The prison holding Dag'draath is breaking. Surely even in the desert the situation has come to your attention?"

She narrowed her eyes, uncrossing her arms as she dropped her hand to her side, fingers beginning to tap rapidly against her right thigh. "Yes," she replied, her tone dropping another several degrees.

I wasn't sure if she was mad at me or the situation. When she abruptly stood and began to pace across the front dais, the leader of the scavengers shifted closer to me. The lump which had been keeping my stomach uncomfortably full shifted to my chest and pressed uncomfortably against my heart.

She stopped pacing and abruptly turned to me.

"So, you want to put him back in his prison? Others have already attempted and failed."

I blinked. This was news to me. Someone else had tried to put the dark god back in his kennel? Before I could think through the wisdom of sharing my thoughts, I blurted out my previously unspoken plan.

"No, I want to break his prison and destroy him for good.

At first, the sharp featured woman blinked at me, her face a blank mask of surprise, then she erupted into gales of laughter. Heat rose in my cheeks, but I waited. This time I didn't glance at my friends for fear I would see the same expression of disbelief on their faces, or worse—terror.

"You are even more foolish than you look, child. Aria and Beru thought they were strong enough, smart enough to trap Dag'draath. At least their plan made sense. But all they achieved for their pains was to make things even worse. Ur'gel are now everywhere, double and triple the amount we were seeing before the dumb duo attempted their futile mission."

I raised my eyebrows. Beru? Could there be more than one? Or could it possibly be the man I'd read about in the Library? The first lieutenant everyone believed had turned traitor and gone over to the dark? I filed the information away for later, taking another step closer to the Sovran to somehow get her to support my case.

"It's obvious the original spell failed. It barely succeeded in trapping him for two centuries, let alone forever the way it was intended. We need a permanent solution and soon. I know if I can find the artifact I discovered in the Library's files, the secret of achieving this will be close at hand. If I find the artifact, I can do it."

Jaydra shook her head, stepping back and returning to sit in her chair. She shook her head as she looked at me, disbelief and disappointment mixing equally on her face. Turning her head, she looked at the leader of the scavenger and nodded once.

"I expected … more. Pity. Throw them into the dungeon."

"Please, Sovran! Don't do this. I'm not making it up. I really do think it's possible. But we need your help, and there's no way we can stop anything from inside a prison."

Rough arms grabbed my wrists as my words fell on deaf ears. I waited without protest as I was tied with the same rough rope from our walk to the Oubliee settlement, completely deflated by my failure to convince her. Jaydra had turned away and was no longer listening, with several advisors now clustered around, blocking her from sight.

Muffled sounds of protest came from my friends at the similar treatment they were receiving as we were led outside the grand hall toward our new quarters, which I suspected I wouldn't enjoy.

If I'd thought finding the Heart Stone in the Northwestern Lands would be a challenge, this added an entirely unexpected level of complexity to our mission. Now the biggest question wasn't how would we find the stone, but how were we going to get out?

CHAPTER 14

The ropes burned my wrists and I knew I'd have chafe marks later. Once I'd resigned myself to the fact Jaydra had turned her back and wouldn't listen to anything else I had to say, I'd gone quietly. Although a dungeon was hardly ideal for planning or achieving our goals, the alternative if I angered her would certainly be worse.

Her sharp featured face and shrewd eyes had warned more clearly than her words had; she was a leader who had no problem ruling by force or fear. If there was a way to make her listen, arguing was not it.

Which was why we allowed ourselves to be led, unprotestingly, toward the ominous-sounding dungeon she'd consigned us to. This time, our young guard led us.

Gwen was beside him, followed meekly by her three wolves. I was in the middle with the lead scavenger keeping a firm grip on both guys. Based on my young servant's expression, it bordered on painful.

Will, of course, had his usual smirk present, but a faint tightening around his eyes told me he was just as uncomfortable.

The building we were walking through appeared to have

been designed as a home and headquarters. It was every bit as large and winding as the castle I'd grown up in, but the aesthetics were different. It had no beautiful tapestries or works of art. Instead, the walls themselves were embellished with engraved archways and ornate mosaic tile work, creating a functional beauty I found as lovely as my own home.

At least until we went down a flight of stairs.

The walls became a plain gray stone, without any decoration save for torch brackets on the walls every few feet. The hallway was lit with an eerie yellow glow, which did nothing to dispel the shadows pooling in the corners.

I shivered. Even above ground with the wind, I hadn't felt cold until now. From the unfamiliar dampness I guessed we must be subterranean. I hoped we didn't have to spend long down here, as the climate didn't feel suitable for maintaining healthy prisoners.

"Enjoy your stay." The lead scavenger spoke for the first time.

I waited as he unbound my wrists, bothered by the cruel smirk on his face. It was obvious he enjoyed putting people in the dungeon. Another chill crept over my back as I recognized the look in his eyes. He also looked like he would enjoy causing pain.

I stepped back, worried he was going to strike me as the look in his eye darkened, becoming menacing. Just as I prepared to defend myself, the younger guard unlocked a large metal door and gestured for us to enter.

Gwen and the wolves went first, and I gratefully followed, eager to escape the evil in the leader's eyes. The guard opened the door to a cage about half the size of the room, and we walked in, followed by Will and Sel. The guard slammed the door shut, leaving without a word. The metal door shut behind him, the ominous clank of a key in the lock echoing in the silent stone chamber.

I looked at my new home and winced. Grey stone walls, the

same as the hallway, although slightly wider. The actual cage they'd placed us in was about twice times my height and at least four times as wide. We had enough space to move around, but not enough to be comfortable if we all tried to lay down at the same time.

As I looked at the single pallet on the floor in the back corner which apparently passed for a bed, it was clear sleeping comfortably was not a requirement for prisoner safety. Exhaling, I crouched and rested my elbows on my knees as I rubbed my forehead.

"Now what?" Gwen placed a soft hand on my shoulder.

I looked at her, placing my hand on top, taking comfort from her strength. "I don't know. I didn't anticipate any of this. Not the near crash-landing, the kidnapping, and definitely not being involuntary guests of a tribe of humans I've only seen referenced in a textbook."

"Yeah, today does put a kink in our plans, doesn't it?" Will's sardonic voice came from the far corner.

Although I was thankful my ropes had been removed before we'd been placed in the cage, I had the overwhelming urge to call the guards back and ask if they could gag him.

I narrowed my eyes. "Yes, it does. Do you have any great ideas, oh wise one?"

He carefully wiped the smirk from his face, shook his head and came to sit beside me, tucking his legs beneath him.

"Look, Rhin. No one's blaming you for what happened. Captain Baeley didn't want to land where she did. It's just how things played out. I don't think anyone could have anticipated the Oubliee coming upon us the way they did. It's always a risk in the border zones. It's a big territory. Even the path we took to get to the village didn't appear to be traveled daily. It's completely possible they only go that way monthly. It just so happens we were there when they came by. Lucky for them, unlucky for us."

He looked at me with a self-deprecating smile and I realized with a start he wasn't trying to deliberately irritate me. It was just his way to lighten the mood.

I closed my eyes and took a deep breath before looking at him. "I'm sorry. I realize I'm taking this personally. Being a prisoner wasn't something I factored into our quest. Death and injury, sure. In fact, I was convinced I was going to die long before we reached the Soul Goblet. But prison?" I shook my head. "Seriously, who takes people prisoner? Dag'draath's forces generally stick to murder and pillaging. And I'm sure if the Library wanted to torture me, it wouldn't do it by locking me up."

I looked at my friends. Will and Gwen were quiet, and their faces were contemplative. When I looked at Sel, however, I was surprised to note he wasn't even listening.

"What are you doing?" I squinted but couldn't see anything out of the expected for a drab cell.

He turned, wrinkling his nose as he answered thoughtfully. "I'm just looking at the room. The metal bars don't look easy to move and they're too narrow for us to slip through. It's also not very well lit, which may be deliberate, but may also provide us with an opportunity to escape, if we can use it to our advantage."

I tilted my head, impressed. "Wow. Here I am, feeling sorry for myself and thinking there's no way in heck we're going to get out of here. Meanwhile, you've been assessing the dungeon for signs of weakness?"

He shrugged one shoulder modestly. "I told you before we left Cliffside, being a servant, or slave, at Cliff Castle taught me a few things about being sneaky. One of those is to remember even the most inconvenient situations can hold hidden opportunities. It's just a matter of looking." He smiled. "If you never look, you won't find anything."

I nodded at his surprisingly mature insight. "Very true. A good thing to keep in mind. Thank you. So, assuming we're able to escape the cage, how are we going to get out of the building? And how do we find the temple? We don't have any landmarks or a guide."

Will bit his lip, shrugging helplessly.

Gwen appeared similarly stymied. "Obviously, the best answer would be to find a guide for the temple," slowly adding, "assuming we can get out of course."

"Assuming," I agreed.

"I was thinking about that. You've got an almost perfect memory for details, don't you? Or am I attributing extra skills to you?" Will wore a pensive expression over his face.

"Yes, one of my abilities is having an almost flawless memory. It's been helpful with studying, but I've used it with directions as well. I rarely get lost somewhere I've been."

He resumed his usual irritatingly satisfied smirk. "Great. So, worst case scenario, if we can escape our cage, you should be able to find the way back through the castle and out the way we came?"

"Probably. But you're forgetting all the guards we'll have to get through. It may be better to find a secondary route which is a little quieter."

His face fell. "Right. Guards."

We sat for moment without speaking as we tried to decide what to do next. Without a plan and without any assistance from the Oubliee, it felt impossible to get out of the cage, let alone find the temple. My mind drifted back to the two-way book I'd used in the temple on Bomrega Island. It had allowed Jarid to pass me information, but I couldn't see a way to leverage him to our benefit under the circumstances we were currently in.

I bit the inside of my cheek, maintaining my crouched position as I thought until my feet fell asleep. I shifted my weight just before I fell over, shaking out my legs and sitting cross-legged beside Gwen.

After a while, Sel stopped pacing around the cage and joined us on the floor.

The wolves were comfortable in the corner, curled up together. They appeared to be napping and were strangely content with the situation. Then again, so far, the Oubliee had been kinder to them than they had been to us.

My suspicions they preferred the wolves to us were confirm ed a few moments later. The young guard returned and threw three chunks of quality raw meat on the floor beside the wolves, then placed four plain containers on the floor just outside the bars. Without speaking, he left again.

Sel grabbed the first bowl.

I knew immediately the contents weren't going to be great when my normally starving and non-picky servant turned his nose up and put the bowl back down.

"That bad?" Gwen winced.

He nodded glumly, looking as depressed as I remembered seeing him.

I wrinkled my nose. "Clearly they like the wolves more. Do you think it's poisoned?"

He shook his head. "It's basically gruel, so I'm not sure why they'd bother. If I prefer starving over it, no one else would touch it."

Despite his warning, my stomach prodded me. It felt like forever since I'd eaten, so I decided to chance it. It had the texture of a sticky, watery porridge, without as much flavor. When I didn't immediately stop eating, Sel took his bowl back and the others braved it as well. I caught a flash of jealously cross Gwen's face as she watched the wolves tear into the meat.

When we were finished, at least my stomach was full, but otherwise we were in the same situation we'd been in a moment earlier. Less hungry, but just as stymied about what to do next.

The door edged open a crack.

We immediately stopped talking, expecting either the young guard, or worse, the leader of the scavengers with the dark and menacing eyes. To my surprise, it was the same woman who'd found us in our previous lock-up.

She peeked around the door, surveying the room. Once she saw we were alone, she stepped in and shut it quietly behind her.

"Wait, how did you get here?" Will stood, walking to the bars of the cage. "What about the guards?"

Nyalla smiled, looking modestly down at the floor as she scuffed the toe of her soft leather shoe against the stone floor. "I know the guard. He allowed me in to visit for a few minutes."

Gwen's eyebrows shot up. "Really? Rather surprising, given your reception by our other captor."

Her face hardened and she curled her lip. "Him? Son of a pig. He is not fit to kiss the dirt at my feet." She emphasized her words by spitting on the floor. "He isn't worth the ground my refuse is dumped on. No, it was not him. He has other, more important things to deal with than prisoners he took from the mountains. The guard I am talking about is the other one, a friend of a friend. It happens I have something he wanted. For a price, he has allowed me speak with you."

I considered her words.

Although she seemed to be on our side and had now shown up twice, I didn't know if we could trust her. No one else had come to aid us, or even listened, though.

"Why are you here?" I stood up, walking the short distance to stand beside Will. "It's a lot of effort and risk for people you don't know. Especially given how we've been treated by everyone else." I crossed my arms and waited for her to convince me.

She inclined her head. "This is true. It isn't without risk for me to be here. But I am willing to help you. For a price."

"A price?" It was Gwen's turn to look suspicious. She leaned her shoulder onto mine, and without thinking I laced my fingers with hers.

Nyalla smiled, like a cat who'd caught a mouse. "My price? Nothing, really. Except if I can get you out of here, you let me come."

"Why would you want to come with us? You don't know us or where we're going."

She brushed my question aside. "The why isn't important. I can tell from looking at you, you're good people. I wish to get out of this village but traveling alone isn't safe. I can help you escape. Surely, my company isn't too much of a price to pay for your freedom?" She raised an eyebrow, looking between us for an answer.

I bit my lip as I considered her proposition. When Sel stepped forward eagerly, I knew what the answer would be. After glancing at the others, I gestured for Will to answer.

"If you can get us out of here, you can come. What's your plan?"

"I know my way through the building, and I have allies. I can get us out of here and past the town wall. There's a route other than the way you entered." She shook her head, her long brown hair reminding me of one of the wild horses from the Low Forest plains.

I didn't trust her motivation. Why would she want to come with us if she could get out of town on her own? But given our lack of alternatives I was willing to accept help, even from an unlikely source. I would've been happier if it was someone I knew and trusted, but beggars couldn't be choosers.

"Let's go." I didn't want to wait.

Jaydra had struck me as a stubborn and savvy woman.

I worried she'd change her mind and call for us. I doubted she'd change her mind and aid us in finding the temple. Which left Nyalla as our best and only chance for escape.

A triumphant smile spread over her face and she turned just as the door opened. The young guard entered, and my heart sank. To my surprise, he handed her a key, turned his back, and walked away.

Within moments, the door to our cage was open and we were free. Even though we hadn't been locked up for long, it was enough to decide I didn't wish to stay a minute longer. I slung my satchel over my shoulder and hurried after our mysterious savior.

CHAPTER 15

Nyalla may have known people but escaping proved more challenging than she'd made it seem. She led us in the opposite direction from which we'd entered the dungeon to another set of stairs which we ascended silently. When we reached the top, she suddenly threw an arm out, gesturing wildly for us to hide behind her.

I looked around frantically for a place; four people and three wolves weren't exactly easy to tuck away. Luckily, the stairs had a circular alcove hidden from the upstairs. I held my breath and tightly pressed back against my friends until she gestured for us to move.

I peered into the hallway as a guard disappeared around the far corner and knew we'd narrowly missed running into him. From then on, I became increasingly tense. It seemed like every single corner we came to, more guards appeared.

Through some miracle, Nyalla always seemed to know when one would appear, and each time we reached another fork in our path, she made us wait as she checked the hall first.

I only realized we'd reached the outer wall of the castle when I saw the sun's light filtering down from high on the wall to my right.

A flutter of hope replaced the bitter acid of adrenaline. Just when I could almost taste freedom, a piercing alarm split the silence.

"Ur'gel balls!" Nyalla cursed.

I blinked. Until now, we'd remained completely silent. Apparently now the alarm had been raised, Nyalla no longer felt it was important to be quiet.

Nyalla looked at the wolves, narrowing her eyes. "We need to leave the wolves behind. We'll be too obvious outside with them."

Gwen's expression instantly flashed from disbelief to anger. "Absolutely not. The wolves come with me at *all* times."

My breath puffed out, knowing we were about to waste time we didn't have. "Look, we appreciate your help, but there's no point arguing. The wolves come with us. Let's get out of here. We can figure the rest out once we're outside."

Nyalla gritted her teeth but nodded. "Fine. The exit is just around this corner. Once you get outside, there's a courtyard. We'll need to scale the wall to get out, but there's a tree with branches. They should reach low enough for you to climb over. Anyone who can't make it won't get out."

Without delay, we followed her around the corner. Standing at the exit was another guard. With the alarm still blaring, he raised his weapon the second he saw us.

He opened his mouth, but Nyalla raised a hand, shushing him before he could speak. "Braydin, stand down."

Nyalla approached him, holding out a hand. Braydin blinked and lowered his sword, his expression turning dreamy when he recognized her.

"Nyalla."

I wasn't sure what their relationship was but based on his expression he wouldn't do anything to stop us long as Nyalla was there. Without waiting to test my theory, I bolted for the door, the footsteps of my friends close behind.

Once in the courtyard, I looked around. It was larger than

expected, but empty except on tree at the far end. It appeared to have grown sideways at one point, and a large branch draped down into the courtyard. I made a beeline for it, glancing back long enough to make sure my friends were still there.

When I saw them close behind, I ran as fast as I could. If I could just climb over, I had no doubt the others would make it as well.

Breathing hard with exertion and fear, I climbed a tree for the first time in my life.

The last branch was about four feet away from the wall, so I paused, taking one more deep breath, and leapt. Landing awkwardly on the edge of the wall, I windmilled my arms to regain my balance, then dropped almost the height of one of the small buildings beside me to the ground below.

One by one, the others joined me. The wolves jumped over, making it look effortless. I wished I had half their grace. The final person over was Nyalla, who seemed remarkably unruffled under the circumstances.

She smiled at Gwen's suspicious glare and immediately turned her attention to the wolves. "If you're not willing to leave them behind, we can't walk around with them looking like that." She gestured to the wolves.

Instantly, I knew what she was talking about. Throughout our travels, they had maintained a striking nobility and cleanliness. Although their fur was varying shades of white, gray, and black, it was so shiny they demonstrated little resemblance to the canine cousins I'd seen on our way through the village. Those had mostly been mutts, and were a dirty brown, either genetically or from the incessant desert winds and sand.

Nyalla pointed out a bucket of water underneath an abandoned clothesline next to the wall. "Make them look dirtier. And quickly. We need to get out of here. Now the alarm has sounded, every guard in the village will be looking for you."

Gwen looked down at the wolves, doubt on her face. They

appeared unperturbed though, and after staring at Swift for a moment, she sighed and dumped the bucket on the ground, stirring the water into the dirt until she'd made a muddy paste.

If I'd ever doubted her connection with her wolves, what happened next would have convinced me they really could speak to each other. First Swift, then Kiya and Damio. One by one, the wolves rolled on the spot the water had been dumped, moving over to allow the next to take their turn. Within seconds, three muddy wolves stood in front of us.

Gwen sighed as she knelt and began to rub the mud into Swift's fur, a pained look on her face as she glanced at me. "Rhin? If you work on Kiya, I think Damio will let Sel fix his mud job. We need to make sure they are evenly covered."

I nodded and knelt beside Kiya, following her lead. I marveled at how patiently the wolves allowed the three of us to complete their disguise. It wasn't perfect, and if anyone looked closely they would be able to tell they weren't ordinary mutts, but already it was far less apparent they were the same animals who'd entered the sovran's castle with the prisoners only hours earlier.

I stood and turned to Nyalla once I was finished, only to be greeted with fabric thrown at my head. "Oomph!" I pulled it away from my mouth, spitting lint out.

"Here, put this on. Your clothing marks you too noticeably as outsiders. Once you're done, we'll separate. We're too obvious in a large group. Quickly!"

I considered the item Nyalla had thrown at me, finding what appeared to be a long dress. It was boring, mud-brown, and difficult to tell whether it was meant to be worn by a male or female. At least it smelled clean, which was more than I could say for my current attire. I pulled it over my head as she threw more of the items from the clothesline at the others.

Once I was dressed, she tossed another piece of fabric to me, this one narrower and longer. I wrapped it around my head the way I'd seen her put on her scarf. It was rough, but I hoped it would pass. Nyalla looked at me and nodded, waiting for the others to be similarly outfitted before she turned to Will, examining him with narrowed eyes.

"You seem bright." She gave him a quick once over. He was almost unrecognizable in his long, gray robe and head covering. "I want you and the female who's so attached to the wolves to take one or two of them. Head south and loop around back after a few hundred paces. You'll see a small one-story building with a blue door. Once you get there, turn left and head straight. That'll take you to a small hut with an outbuilding right next to the wall. We'll meet up there. Don't speak with anyone. If you see any guards, head the other direction. Do not engage with *anyone*."

He nodded. "We don't have any weapons. That's gonna be a problem."

Nyalla shook her head. "I'll see what I can do, but don't count on anything. They took your weapons before you even got to the village. I know of one place on the way out where some of the scavenging is kept. I can look but may not have a chance to liberate anything. It's more important to get to the other side of the wall before nightfall."

He nodded, his uneasiness at being unarmed against the Oubliee visible as he shifted his weight from foot to foot.

Nyalla turned to Sel and I. "You two will come with me. You look less useful and you'll need my help if the guards catch us."

Sel frowned and crossed his arms.

I was irritated at her blunt assessment but didn't argue. I couldn't deny it was an accurate assessment. Will was a trained soldier and Gwen had been hunting with her wolves for years. I had basically been a pampered princess until I left Cliffside and Sel was my loyal manservant. If anyone needed help, it would likely be us.

"Fine," I casted a longing glance at Gwen. I didn't want to let her out of my sight, but I knew It was just my feelings getting in the way. Nyalla had divided the group in a way I could appreciated as being tactically sensible. "Can we at least attempt to get weapons before we leave?"

Nyalla bit her lip. "Maybe. We'll play it by ear. Don't talk, keep your heads down, and the wolves better act like injured dogs if anyone comes near. Most of the strays around here have been thoroughly tamed, so they're unlikely to act aggressive or challenge anyone."

I saw a muscle twitch in Gwen's jaw before she reluctantly nodded. She crouched down. Swift met her eyes and I watched as they communicated silently.

After a moment, Swift licked her face before coming to stand beside me, hunching his powerful shoulders in a way which changed his entire appearance to timid as leaned on my leg.

I could swear he was enjoying acting. When he winked at me, I was sure of it.

"Rhin, Swift is going to go with you guys to keep you safe. Kiya and Damio will come with us."

"Good. Now, go. We'll go this way." Nyalla pointed to the left and we went right. Everything within me screamed this was a bad idea, but what choice did we have? I turned my head as they slipped out of sight.

Nyalla proved to be as slippery as a shadow, leading us on a zigzagging path through back alleys. Whenever we'd encounter someone, she'd find another alley. Everywhere we looked, it seemed as if guards and locals were searching for us, but even if they spotted us, their alert eyes passed us without recognition.

Occasionally, someone would see Nyalla and she'd wave cheerily as she kept moving. I kept my scarf firmly over my face and avoided eye contact while Sel, used to being invisible as a servant, followed silently behind us.

The alarm was still sounding an earsplitting, high-pitched wail, but thankfully it only blared out every few minutes. We focused all our energy on moving as rapidly as possible without running. I was too scared to have questions and Nyalla made no effort to reassure as she guided us on a winding path through town.

My heart leapt at the large stone wall rising in front of us. But instead of heading straight for it as I expected, Nyalla veered to the right. For a moment, I was certain she was leading us into a trap, but when I saw a building beside a locked cage, I knew this was the place she'd mentioned earlier. My heart leapt at the thought of retrieving our confiscated belongings until I noticed the guards. I almost told her to forget it, but I didn't want to chance anyone overhearing me and hesitated.

Nyalla put her arm on my arm, holding her other hand out. We stopped with Swift close at my side, alert and watchful as she pointed first at herself, then at our belongings. I knew she meant for us to stay while she attempted to grab things and I winced, unsure of the risk. Noticing my uncertainty, she narrowed her eyes and glared. I shrugged, and she turned away. As gracefully as a dancer, she slipped over to the small building.

An interminably long time later, she returned with Will's sword, one of Gwen's knives, and the knife I'd been using since the first ur'gel attack. When I tilted my head, impressed despite myself, she merely winked and gestured for us to follow her.

By now, guards were everywhere. I was glad we hadn't gone toward the main gate, as I was certain they had been barricaded. Nyalla didn't seem worried, continuing to slip through alleyway after alleyway as we tried to keep up.

Trying not to pant, my breath caught in my throat when I saw the others hiding behind a shed by the outer wall.

Nyalla locked eyes with Will, then jerked her head to the left before continuing toward the shed.

Once we reached their position, Nyalla looked both ways

before creeping forward and opening the door to a small, battered house. The moment we entered, she relaxed and threw off her headscarf. Looking around, it was easy to see this was her home. It was small, without many personal touches, but looked lived in. The most interesting feature I could see was a door on the back wall.

For the first time since our escape had begun, she looked at us and spoke in a low voice. "Do not speak, say nothing. We may be safe here, or we may not. The door you see behind you is a hidden exit to the town. No one else knows about it and I want to keep it that way. Grab those packs, put them on, and follow me. We're about to go into the heart of the desert, and you will need everything I have placed in those bags."

I looked over to where she was pointing, seeing four large, leather packs which appeared to have been stuffed full. I lifted the one closest to me, grunting with the effort. Once I had slipped it on my back, the straps on my shoulders allowed it to sit comfortably and distributed the weight well enough I didn't notice it as much. I moved my satchel in front of my body, grateful once more no one else seemed to realize the value inside.

The others quickly placed a bag on their backs and the moment we were loaded up, Nyalla opened the plain wooden door. We slipped out behind her as the sound of alarms echoed around us.

CHAPTER 16

It was as if we had walked into another world. The sky had darkened around us but in no way did nightfall obstruct our view of the desert. I had no clue how Nyalla managed to hide her secret entrance, and the more suspicious part of me couldn't help wondering why she wanted to come with us if she had such easy access to the desert. But suspicions aside, our other options were exceedingly limited. Without a guide, supplies, and especially without her assistance leaving both the prison and the town, there was no way we would've made it as far as we had.

I looked at the others. Were they were feeling the same mix of emotions as I was? Gwen caught my eye and a smile blossomed across her beautiful face. In all the excitement, our stolen moments together on the ship seemed so long ago. The look in her eyes promised me nothing had changed, and I held out my hand, grateful when she accepted it.

We stood together, fingers laced, and waited as Nyalla squinted into the oncoming night. When she turned abruptly, I was surprised by what she had to say.

"The desert is dangerous, even for those who know it well. It is far too hot to travel comfortably during the day, so we need to keep moving to reach a shelter before dawn, and not just in case the Oubliee come looking for you."

Will nodded, hoisting his bag higher on his back as he straightened his shoulders. "Do you know where we're going?"

I inwardly winced at the look of admiration on his face. Was I about to watch Will try to put some of his relationship advice into action? I couldn't blame him though—she was a beautiful woman, if a little old for him. Perhaps if the situation was different, I would have had a case of hero worship myself.

Nyalla pointed off in the distance, but all I could see was sand and clouds when I followed her hand. "There's a place, about eight hours from here. We can rest there for the day. It's a cave system, known only to those familiar with the desert."

"Would those people include the Oubliee?" Gwen's eyes narrowed.

I wasn't sure if it was suspicion I saw, or her merely attempting to see what Nyalla had been pointing toward.

"Yes, which means we must be careful. I imagine they'll assume you will be unable to get out of the city for at least another day. By the time they think to check beyond the walls, I'm hopeful we'll have a significant head start. They wouldn't set out in the daytime in the desert for the likes of you."

Her words stung, but as I considered them, I realized she was likely correct. After all, what were we other than spoils of salvage? It wasn't as if we were long-standing enemies or important prisoners. I may have tried to petition their leader for help, but I hadn't told her what we were looking for, had I? I couldn't remember, which bothered me. Trying to push my niggling uncertainty aside, I spoke up.

"It sounds like a reasonable plan. Do you know if this is the right direction for where we need to search? We are looking for an item I believe was hidden in the middle of the Desert of Souls. The only problem is all of my maps show lush vegetation, and none of this was there at the time it was hidden."

I looked around at the flat, barren landscape which was

quickly cooling off as the suns set. I told myself the environment was the reason for the chill which crossed my spine and made me shiver.

"While I'm not certain what it is you seek, we are on the periphery of the Northwestern Lands currently and the Desert of Souls is deeper within these territories. The shelter I have in mind is in the vicinity of where you're headed, if not right next to it. The Desert of Souls is further in. Once we reach the caves, we can discuss the details further."

I nodded, looking at my companions.

Will appeared as if he would gladly follow her to the ends of Lynia, and the reassuring squeeze of Gwen's hand in mine told me all I needed to know about her willingness to come with me.

Sel caught my eye, dipping his head in a faint echo of servitude from home, a time which seemed like years ago now. Seeing we were all in agreement to carry on, we followed Nyalla deeper into the Northwestern Lands.

OVER THE NEXT FEW HOURS, I became even more grateful for our disguise than I had been when we'd been attempting to escape the Oubliee.

We'd worn it to disguise who we were at that point and now we used it to hide from the brutal winds.

I had thought they were bad when we'd been led single file from the mountain range to the village, but the intensity now was double that experience. If it hadn't been for the scarf and rough clothing I wore on top of mine, my face would have been rubbed raw.

As it were, my teeth were full of grit and my eyes burned, tearing perpetually in a futile attempt to moisten themselves.

Nyalla seemed to be a brilliant guide, knowing unerringly which direction to travel in a landscape which was unending and undifferentiated to me. At least, I hoped she was. There was no way for me to tell if we were lost or not, other than the fact she was satisfied with our progress.

She allowed us to stop a few times for short breaks whenever there was a sheltered alcove, and I was pleasantly surprised to find she'd packed not only water, but also dried food in each pack. It was almost as if she'd done this before, which again made me wonder why she'd wanted us to bring her along. From everything I could tell, she obtained little benefit in exchange for taking a huge risk on us.

"Is everything okay, Rhin?" Nyalla was looking at me curiously, her face open and friendly.

She'd taken off the headscarf to eat, and we'd all followed suit. With the rocky ledge we'd tucked ourselves into, it was a break from the wind and the stifling heat of the material.

Shame filled me. I didn't know when I'd become so guarded and suspicious about someone's motives. I couldn't help but feel the Library was telling me to be careful, but at her question, I felt ungrateful and rushed to reassure her.

"Yes, everything is fine." I lifted a shoulder, making a show of wiping a bead of sweat off my face as I gave her a smile. "I guess I'm tired. I'm not used to how fierce the winds are."

Nyalla nodded sympathetically, pressing her lips together. "They are why people mostly stay within the village walls. Unless you're a scavenger or have business at one of the other villages, no one enters the deserts voluntarily."

Gwen narrowed her eyes, moving closer to where I sat. "So why are you out in the desert?"

Her words were clipped, and a little abrupt, but Nyalla didn't take offense.

"Because they don't treat me very well there," she said, gazing back in the direction of the village before shaking her head. "I'm not from there, originally. I have no family, and after my betrothed died, I had nowhere else to go."

Gwen looked at me, a stricken expression on her face.

I could tell she felt sorry she'd dredged up bad memories,

but I wondered if maybe she was acting so harsh with Nyalla for the same reason I was uncomfortable—because we both felt there was more to our mysterious helper than simple benevolence at play.

Will sat beside Nyalla, cautiously putting an arm around her.

Nyalla put her hand on the one he had placed on her shoulder and patted it briefly before she stood and looked down at us all.

Interesting.

She hadn't rejected him exactly, but neither had she actively encouraged him.

"It was all such a long time ago. Most of the sorrow has faded, but unfortunately, I discovered shortly after moving the village where the Oubliee lived would never be my home."

She began repacking her bag as we waited for her to tell us more, curious what she would say next. But to my dismay, when she finished packing, she turned and pointed toward the caves again.

"It's time to go. It will be daylight soon and we don't want to be exposed when it gets hot. If you think the sand and wind is bad now, you are not prepared for how the sun can burn you alive."

I wasn't excited about the possibility of worse weather but didn't complain. In minutes we'd repacked and were on our way again. Except for the harsh climate, I think I would've found the walk enjoyable. The stars in the desert sparkled and although it was dark, they lit our way, highlighting the stark beauty of the barren land.

Before much longer, a large outcropping of rocks became visible, jutting from the ground as if a building had been dropped in the middle of nowhere.

When Nyalla spotted them, she smiled. "We're almost there. In the rocky terrain ahead are the caves where we'll spend the day resting."

I looked at the horizon and my breath caught as the sky appeared to catch on fire as the sun rose in the distance. It looked enormous against the desolate landscape. My mouth was dry by this time, and my flask was as well.

We'd drank almost all the water Nyalla had packed and I hoped she had an idea where to find more. I knew we could go sometime without food, but I thought it quite unlikely we'd be able to make it for long without liquids.

When we finally began to pick our way through rocks, part of me was disappointed to find she hadn't exaggerated about it being a set of small caves. While far from roomy, and with nothing but sand for our beds, the shelter provided enough protection for us to unwind our scarves and cloaks and place them beneath us. Once accomplished, we swiftly fell asleep from exhaustion.

THE NEXT NIGHT, we woke at dusk and ate quickly. Nyalla had solved the issue of our near depleted water supply on waking by taking one of the long sticks from the floor of the cave and digging down into the center of the room. It looked like magic to me. The way she'd used a forked stick to guide her to a dig site, and water had been there? Maybe anyone could do it, but it amazed me.

Seeing my look of bewilderment, she grinned. "The water table is just below ground. That's why no one can live out here. On one hand, the sand and sun are too powerful to support life, but on the other, it's almost impossible to dig any distance down to construct buildings without flooding the area and wasting the limited water resources. But for travelers such as ourselves, it provides just enough water to keep us moving toward the next oasis."

Impressed with Nyalla's resourcefulness, I made a mental note of her trick. I'd never read anything about finding water in that fashion in any book I'd ever read. I drank my fill and topped up my flask after the others took their fill. Once satiated, we followed Nyalla into the desert again.

We fell into an easy rhythm, with Will walking beside Nyalla and Sel a few paces behind. I watched as they talked, observing Will on his most charming behavior.

Gwen and I finally had a chance to spend time together. For the most part we walked quietly. Just being near her was enough to cause my heart to sing. Sel seemed to be okay, his normal, silent self as he gazed at the landscape and eavesdropped from his spot in the middle of the group.

The next day, Nyalla helped us build a fire. This time, our shelter was a sandy outcropping near a rocky dune. It didn't have the benefit of a roof, the way the caves had, but she showed us a type of dried twig-like shrub, the same one which had rolled across the sand and accompanied us during our trek made a suitable kindling. Both Gwen and Sel were fascinated and barraged her with questions.

As I watched them, the key on my chest felt warm. It seemed to almost pulse, making its presence known and as it did, the same uncertainty about Nyalla rose again. Perhaps it was merely jealousy. I watched Gwen laugh at something and tried to brush the thoughts away. But the suspicion bothered me. Which was worse? If I was jealous, or the key was trying to warn me Nyalla was not all she seemed?

Will, of course, had an almost dreamy expression on his face as Nyalla talked.

I rolled my eyes when he passed her some brush.

Gwen noticed and frowned before coming to sit beside me. "Is everything okay?" She kept her voice low as she searched my eyes.

I forced a smile. "Yes, of course." I pressed my lips together, not wanting to divulge my foolish insecurities.

She tilted her head and looked at me, her eyes warm and inviting. "What's going on? I've never seen you act so hot and cold before." She bit her lip, pausing as they widened. "I didn't do anything, did I?"

I shook my head, putting my hand on top of the one she'd placed on my knee when she'd sat next to me. Tiny sparks of electricity seemed to shoot between us. I felt the heat warm my cheeks as her touch affected me the same way it had since the ship.

"No, it's not you. I don't know. I just..." I bit the inside of my cheek, letting my gaze wander to where the boys sat laughing at something Nyalla said. When I looked back at Gwen, comprehension had replaced her worried expression.

"Something about her, isn't it? On the one hand, she's been extremely helpful, and nothing but friendly. And yet..."

Relief swept over me as I realized she had the same reservations I did. I leaned closer, bringing my lips to her ears. "I don't trust her motivation but now I'm wondering how much of my ill will is jealousy."

I watched as the point of her ear lifted and was filled with the urge to nibble on it. I blinked and managed to stop before I did. Our relationship hadn't progressed to public displays of affection, and I wasn't sure how she felt about biting.

Our faces were now only a few inches apart and I saw a flush highlighting the porcelain skin of her cheeks as she took a shuddering breath. Her eyes darkened. "You don't need to be jealous of her. I only have eyes for you."

I leaned closer, about to take her up on the clear invitation I was receiving when Sel's head popped up beside mine.

"Is everything okay here?" His eyes were wide and his face so open I forced my irritation down and smiled reassuringly as I pulled back from Gwen. He was becoming quite observant but had sadly missed the private signals between us.

"Everything is fine. I'm tired from all the walking and the sand, of course, but otherwise doing well. We were just talking about how lucky we are Nyalla knows so much about the Northwestern Lands and the Desert of Souls."

I could tell he didn't completely believe me, but he didn't press. Unfortunately, Will's ears perked up at Nyalla's name and he nodded emphatically.

"I've never met a woman who knew so much before," he gave her an appreciative glance.

Nyalla chuckled. "If you'd lived here as long as I have, you'd know a thing or two as well." She brushed his praise aside easily, but I could see she was pleased at his words.

A yawn escaped me unexpectedly and I clapped my hand over my mouth. "Oh dear! I'm sorry. Apparently, I'm more tired than I realized." I looked longingly at the ground sheet we'd put out to avoid becoming any dirtier while sleeping.

Gwen stood and extended her hand to me, smiling. "Why don't we try to catch some sleep?"

"That's a good idea. But we should take turns standing watch. That way, we won't be surprised by wild animals or the Oubliee if they've managed to catch up with us." Nyalla looked around, shrugging. "As you can see, we're far more exposed here than at the caves when we stopped to sleep last time."

"Absolutely," Gwen agreed. "Do you think we need two at a time?"

We all looked at Nyalla, who narrowed her eyes as she considered the question, before finally shaking her head. "No, it's probably fine to have one guard at a time."

"I can take first watch if you want. I'm not tired yet," Will offered.

"Fine with me. Wake me up when it's my turn. But give me a few hours first. I can hardly keep my eyes open." I muffled another yawn.

Gwen gently led me over to the rough sheet on the ground which would serve as our bed, and I happily curled up against her shoulder with the wolves providing comfortable, cushioned heaters that swiftly lulled me to sleep.

CHAPTER 17

I woke to the sound of muffled conversation. At first, I couldn't remember where I was. The soft feel of fur next my face reminded me I'd been sleeping beside Gwen. The wolves were still there, but she was missing.

Will must've woken her up for watch. That was probably who I'd heard. But as I listened, I realized something strange was going on. I sat up, spotting Sel sleeping beside Damio. Gwen's youngest wolf had become fond of him, and I smiled at the two snuggling before looking toward the fire.

Both Will and Gwen were beside it and Nyalla's sleeping form was a few feet away on another ground cloth.

Gwen cast a glance over and caught me watching them. She gestured for Will to follow and crept over to where I was sitting. I waited, motionless, my sense of curiosity and confusion from waking up to such a strange interaction making me almost think I was dreaming.

She knelt beside me and in a low voice told me what happened. "I don't know what to do," she looked between us. "Will woke me for my turn to be the watch, but when it was my turn to hand it over to Nyalla, she started talking funny, saying she was someone completely different."

I looked at her, my eyebrows shooting up. "What?"

She blew out a long breath, running her fingers through her hair in an abrupt, frustrated gesture. "I know it sounds crazy. I didn't know what to do, so I told her I'd made a mistake and it wasn't her turn yet. She went back to sleep, but he heard us talking and woke up. I was just telling him when I noticed you were awake. Something was different about her. I just don't know what."

I examined him, trying to determine if he believed what she was saying after his earlier efforts to woo Nyalla, and was surprised to see a similarly confused, worried look on his face.

"I'm not sure I would have believed her ... except I caught the tail end of it." He shook his head, brow furrowed, looking almost as bothered as her.

"What do you mean, she was acting different?"

"Well, for starters, she told us her name was something else. Y'serra someone? And her voice was different, less throaty; more musical." She screwed her face up as she recalled it. "It's almost like she was a different person. It still doesn't make sense."

As she struggled to understand what she'd seen, I thought of something I'd read. The name was there, just on the tip of my tongue if I could just remember where I'd read it. Nyalla stirred beside the fire. Gwen's eyes widened with fright.

When I looked over, Nyalla's eyes caught mine. I knew instantly even if she hadn't heard what we'd been discussing, she was awake and aware we were having a conversation.

"Is it my turn yet?"

The sound of her voice made something inside me turn cold and still. It was exactly like they'd said, it was different. While I would describe it as musical and soothing, it was not the same voice I'd become accustomed to.

"No, they came to wake me up for my turn. You can go back to sleep."

She raised an eyebrow. "Are you sure? You seemed quite tired earlier."

I shook my head as I gestured for her to lay down, then shot a warning look at Will and Gwen. "No, I'm fine now. Everyone else should go to sleep. You'll need your strength for traveling tonight."

The other two reluctantly followed my lead, curling up on the sleeping pallet with Sel and the wolves. Nyalla had chosen to sleep on her own, which is why she was on the other side of the fire. At the time, I hadn't thought it was strange. Now I wondered if the reason I'd been feeling so uncertain of her motives was tied to why she'd kept herself at a distance.

As I sat by myself in front of the fire, bits and pieces of what I remembered about the name Y'serra came back. The key around my neck began to pulse a familiar warning, so I focused with diligence. Y'serra, Gwen had said. When Nyalla had spoken in a voice so unlike hers, it had suddenly come back to me.

It was a name I'd only seen once, in an old writing about the Dark War. She'd been known as the Great Betrayer and was the reason Onen Suun had chosen to sacrifice himself in the first place. The book explained it was when she had abandoned him on the eve of their wedding, he had chosen to sacrifice the nine dragons to defeat and imprison Dag'draath. It was the final magic which had supposedly also imprisoned Beru and destroyed this land.

I looked out into the daylight, recalling the history books describing this land as a lush paradise, and saw nothing but sand and emptiness by the harsh light bleaching the desert. How much was true, I wasn't sure, but it was generally agreed at one point, Y'serra had been Onen Suun's betrothed and beloved. Her defection had directly preceded his disappearance and Dag'draath's imprisonment.

I had no idea how long I sat there, staring into the fire while I let my brain work on answers. I was grateful my memory was as good as it was, but at times like this, I wished it was even better. Perhaps if I knew more, I could tie Y'serra to Nyalla.

I knew I wouldn't be able to sleep anymore, but I woke Nyalla after I thought I'd been awake for a few hours. It would have been strange if she didn't have a turn, and at least this way, I'd be able to watch her from the sleeping mat. Then Sel would have the last shift which usually meant a good breakfast. He was the best cook amongst us.

I no longer felt comfortable allowing her to be our sole watcher while the rest of us slept. Hopefully, I could discuss a plan with the others to avoid that happening again without her overhearing.

Even though I hadn't been sure I trusted her before, I'd made the mistake of letting down my guard around her for no reason other than she'd been so kind and so helpful. Now I'd heard the name Y'serra, I'd never be completely able to trust her again. If she could betray her love for the dark one, we could never be truly safe with her.

Nyalla woke easily, her eyes blinking open as she smiled. She sat up and stretched, giving a dainty yawn before standing. "Any concerns? Did you hear or see anything outside the fire ring?"

I shook my head, noticing her voice was back to normal. There was no evidence it had ever sounded different. Had it been a dream? No, others had heard it as well.

I refocused on her question. "No, nothing happened except … well, it's nothing. Let me know if you need anything. It's Sel's turn next, and I'd recommend waking him before you get hungry." I forced a smile, trying to act normal. "He's a great cook."

Nyalla nodded and took my place beside the fire, poking it with the long stick she'd taken from the cave. After using it for finding water, she had decided it was useful and had been using it to poke things and walk with as well. "I certainly can. Enjoy your rest, see you soon."

I waved a hand as I walked over to the others, forcing my eyes to remain on the ground in front of me.

She sounded and acted as if nothing had happened.

I planned to ask her about it as soon as the others were awake, but not yet.

We needed to know what we were up against, and the best way to do that was to make sure we were all there when she explained herself.

I rolled over, assuming a position allowing me to keep my eye on her without her noticing and waited for dusk to fall.

ALTHOUGH I'D BEEN on edge for her shift, Nyalla didn't do anything suspicious. She merely sat by the fire, which was unnecessary save for the fact we'd use it to cook with before we departed and stared into the desert.

How could she possibly be Y'serra? She would be several hundred years old, and she didn't look much older than her mid-twenties. Hardly someone who would have been around during the Dark War, unless there was magic at play.

I was in the process of beating myself up about not knowing more about her back story when she came and gently shook Sel awake. I'd only had about four hours of sleep, but I knew it would be impossible to sleep any longer right now.

It was hard enough sleeping during the day, but once one added in the distraction of a traveling companion who could potentially be the second evilest villain in the history of Lynia, sleep eluded me entirely, even after she'd switched with Sel.

After trying a little longer, I gave up and joined him at the fire. I debated telling him what had happened during the night while helping with breakfast but decided to wait until everyone was awake.

Once we had the food was ready, we woke everyone.

The wolves left under instructions to return within the hour.

I wasn't sure if they were hunting, or just bored and needed a chance to roam freely, but they'd returned every night prior to our journey through the desert, so I wasn't worried.

"Man, I wish you were in the barracks with us. You could get a job as the mess cook, no problem." Will's mouth was full of food as he spoke, but his intentions were clear as he went back for seconds.

Sel gave a modest smile before returning for his own seconds.

Although our water stores had been low, the amount of food Nyalla had packed in each bag should be enough for us without needing to hunt for at least a week. When I'd told her where I thought the temple was, she'd been confident she knew the general location and had promised it should only take us about that long.

To be on the safe side though, Gwen had the wolves bring back some of wild game they found. Due to the more unfamiliar terrain she had relieved us of our hunting duties, which I was grateful for.

"I'm a Low Forest hunter. Although the general principles are the same, the wolves will do a better job in unfamiliar territory by instinct, and I'm not trying to torture you into usefulness the same way I was when you were a sheltered princess-scholar."

I would've taken offense except immediately after she delivered her announcement, her eyes had heated. I knew she was thinking of our stolen kisses and lingering touches when no one else was around.

It was a good thing we wanted to develop a relationship slowly, because otherwise, we both would've been frustrated beyond belief.

We slept in a giant pile, so even though my skin burned

from the proximity to her each time we laid down, our embraces were chaste and fully clothed when anyone else was near, which seemed to always be the case.

Will sighed as he leaned back, patting his stomach with an expression of satisfaction. "You are a surprisingly good cook. Especially considering the tools you have to work with."

Nyalla added her own vote of approval, although she'd stopped with only one portion. I understood why Will needed more, as he was a lot bigger than the rest of us, but it was an eternal mystery to me where Sel put any of the food he ate. His skinny status had only been emphasized further by our travels.

When everyone was in a comfortable and relaxed frame of mind and the sun was setting beautifully in the distance, I decided it was an appropriate time to chance asking Nyalla about what we'd seen during our daytime rest.

"Nyalla," I began, then hesitated. I caught Gwen's expression and I knew she was worried about what I would say next. But it needed to be discussed prior to reaching the lost temple. If Nyalla did mean us harm, I didn't want to hand her anything which could make her more powerful.

"Yes?" Nyalla's voice carried an edge of impatience.

I realized I hadn't finished my sentence, instead letting myself trail off in thought. I shook my head and gave her an apologetic smile. "Sorry, I forgot what I was going to ask for a moment. It's back now."

Nyalla looked curious but unworried, unlike Will and Gwen, who were both tightlipped and fidgeting.

"When you were sleeping, you woke up before it was your turn for watch. You were acting funny."

Nyalla raised her eyebrows. "Funny? I'm not sure I know what you mean."

Sel frowned and I remembered he'd slept through the episode. For his benefit, I reviewed. "When Gwen and Will were trading off the watch, you woke up and started to talk." When Nyalla leaned forward, shrugging her shoulders,

I continued. "You were talking to them, but you sounded like a completely different person. When they said your name, Nyalla, you told them you were someone named Y'serra."

Her eyes widened but before she could object, Gwen cut her off.

"Yes, you seemed to know who we were, but you were very insistent you weren't Nyalla. You were … different." she crossed her arms, lowering her head as she watched Nyalla's reaction.

Nyalla turned to Will and when he nodded in confirmation, she sighed. "I'm sorry. I was really hoping that wouldn't happen again. In fact, it's why I was being careful to sleep a little apart from the rest of you."

She gave us a half smile, allowing her eyes to linger on Will as she directed the next words seemingly to him. "I didn't want you to think any less of me, but my whole life I've felt this strange connection to Y'serra." She looked down, shaking her head as if reliving a painful memory before she looked at me again.

"I don't know why or how it happens, but sometimes I lose time. I can't always tell what I've done or where I've been. Sometimes I get the sensation I'm dreaming when it happens, but other times, I have big gaps in my memory. I'm afraid one of these times, I won't wake up again and this other person, Y'serra, will take over completely."

"Who's Y'serra?" Will asked.

When I looked at the equally perplexed Gwen and Sel, I realized I was probably the only one who would have encountered her name. It made sense. The Dark War had been hundreds of years ago and even I, a scholar who'd researched them extensively since the attacks had begun, still had a tough time finding accurate information and only knew bits and pieces.

"Y'serra was known more commonly during the Dark War

as the Great Betrayer," I earned shocked looks from the others and another ashamed expression from Nyalla.

"It's true. I can't help it though. I don't know why it happens. Maybe I'm a descendant of hers, or maybe it's for another reason. It's why I've keep myself apart from others and why I wanted to leave my home with the Oubliee. I'm never sure what will happen. I don't know if I'm merely dreaming, or if she's controlling me.

"My biggest fear is someday she'll take over my life completely and use it for evil. In fact, it's why I'm helping you. I'm hoping if you can remove the threat of the dark one returning, my curse will be lifted as well. Surely, if the greatest evil in Lynia is removed even if my nightmare comes true, there's nothing she can do to hurt anyone."

I frowned as I watched her. She looked heartbroken and sincere in every way that mattered.

Will clearly believed her story and as Nyalla sat with her face downcast and allowed a few beautiful tears to trail down her cheek, I couldn't blame him. He patted her hand and offered her a cloth to wipe her face.

Sel looked like he didn't know what to believe, but his eyes softened at her desperation.

Gwen's eyebrows were narrowed in a way that made me think she wasn't immune either.

"Well, I for one believe you." Will gently grasped her chin and brought her face to his, searching her eyes as he waited for her reaction.

Nyalla gave him a watery smile and his face softened even further.

Oh man, he's so far gone he'd believe everything she said. I knew she'd won him over. Sel also appeared willing to accept what she'd told us at face value. Maybe it was because of her beauty, or maybe it was because the boys were more trusting.

But I didn't. For reasons unknown even to myself, I couldn't push away the feeling she wasn't telling us the truth.

As I watched the soft and consoling conversation between Nyalla and the others, I knew I needed to keep my suspicions to myself until I had more evidence.

It may not be safe to have her lead us to the temple, but without any other options I would go along with the plan for now and pretend to believe her along with the others.

CHAPTER 18

From then on, I kept a close watch on Nyalla. I couldn't trust her intentions since she'd spoken in a voice so different from her own. I wasn't sure how the others felt, but I didn't speak of it again, especially to the guys.

They appeared to have accepted her explanation wholeheartedly. Will was completely besotted and spent as much time with her as he could, with Sel never more than a pace behind.

He wasn't watching her with the same hero worship he'd displayed for Loglan, but I thought it came a close second.

Each night in the desert was a copy of the day before. With only the vaguest of directions, we followed Nyalla like lambs. I was hesitant to tell her everything I knew after her Y'serra interlude, even at the risk of our journey taking longer.

She might be completely innocent, but if she was Y'serra, it put an entirely different spin on things. It also could why the key around my neck thrummed with what I felt was a warning occasionally, and always while in her presence.

It had been several days since we'd left the settlement, and we'd had no further appearances from Y'serra since.

Nyalla had consistently been herself, even though I'd watched for even the smallest break in character.

I felt alone in my concerns, so I kept them to myself.

Even Gwen had seemingly forgotten or forgiven the odd encounter.

We had just stopped for a midnight snack, Will and Nyalla sitting a short distance away from Gwen and I while Sel played with Damio.

"Rhin, Will just told me you're looking for the Heart Stone. Why didn't you say something sooner?"

I looked up, surprised to find Nyalla standing in front of me with her arms crossed and an irritated scowl.

I gritted my teeth, silently as I silently cursing Will and thought about what to say. I'd need to have a word with him later. I could have sworn we weren't going to tell her about the stone unless absolutely required.

"Yes, I read something about it in Abrecem Secer." I hoped if I left it vague, she'd lose interest about why I was looking for it.

Nyalla shook her head, making a tsking sound. "I wish you'd mentioned it sooner. I could've saved us at least a night of travel. The temple I was taking you to is the wrong one. There's two out here, but few people know of the second one."

"What do you mean, there's two?" Gwen asked, narrowing her eyes at Nyalla before turning to raise an eyebrow in my direction.

I knew she was going to want answers from me later, but luckily, she turned when Nyalla answered.

Nyalla nodded. "Yes, sister temples. The one I was taking you to is more well-known, which is usually where visitors want to go. But from what I understand it's also harder to find since the desert took over. The temple you want, at least the last place the Heart Stone was seen, is the temple of Mahimān-bita Sūrya. It means we'll have to backtrack a little, but we could get there tomorrow if we change course now."

I sighed. I still wasn't convinced it was a promising idea for her to know what we were doing, but it was irritating she'd known all along where we needed to go, and my suspicions had likely prolonged our sandy, windy torture.

"I'm sorry." To my surprise, I meant it. I still didn't trust her, but I was looking forward to getting to the temple and finding the stone. If telling her meant we arrived sooner, I hoped it was for the best. "I didn't realize it would make a difference. I'd only ever read about one temple."

She waved a hand. "It's okay. I should've been more specific. I was so eager to get out of town I didn't ask many questions. When you wanted to go to a temple in the desert, I thought you meant the one everyone knows about. And, well, I understand if you don't trust me." She shrugged, letting a rueful smile spread over her face. "I'm not sure I would trust me either after what I told you the other day."

Great, now I was the jerk. I could tell from the expression on the guys faces they agreed with my silent estimation, even though neither came right out and said it.

Will came to stand next to Nyalla, smiling at her. "I didn't realize you didn't know, or I would've told you sooner. You know I trust you, right? It's not your fault you have a connection with Y'serra."

She batted her eyelashes, glancing down. The gesture hid her eyes and caused her to look like nothing other than a bashful, innocent young woman.

Gag. I was about to chalk my hesitation and distrust up to jealousy until the key around my neck warmed ever so slightly, as if reminding me of its presence. It was like it knew I was on the verge of believing Nyalla and was telling me not to be lulled into a false sense of security. Well, at least I wasn't the only one on guard around her.

I glanced at Gwen. What did she think? We hadn't had an opportunity to speak privately about the Nyalla-Y'serra dichotomy, and after this recent revelation about the temple, it wouldn't surprise me if Gwen believed her as well.

For now, I'd keep my uneasiness to myself. It did no good to alienate the others and practically speaking, we were already at her mercy if she was planning something. I'd never felt more insecure surrounded by my friends, though outwardly everything appeared fine.

We packed quickly once we'd finished eating. To our great relief we only had a few hours to go until our next stop. It was nighttime as always, so we had little way of knowing where we were going other than Nyalla seemed as confident as always in her directions following the light of the moons through the never-ending sea of sand.

So, when I saw trees and scrub appear just over the next sand dune. At first, I thought it was a mirage. When Sel waved for us to look, I knew it wasn't my imagination. Trees and even grass shimmered in front of us as a silver mirror sparkled under the watchful moons.

Water!

My heart leapt at the beauty laid out in the dim light before us.

Nyalla turned to us and smiled. "The sun is just beginning to rise in the east and we probably could walk a distance more, but we'll stay here today." She gestured toward the enticing bounty in front of us. "It's one of the few places in the Northwestern Lands with actual trees. It sits on a firm bedrock with a large underground water source and one of the few above ground lakes in the area, although it is too small to be considered a lake anywhere else. We can replenish our supplies here and best of all, we can get transportation to make the rest of the trip go faster."

She gave us a smug look at our gasps of astonishment. "I'd planned to come here anyway, so we aren't too far off track of where I would have taken us had I known which temple you had intended to go. We need to resupply here but now our next stop will be the temple if we can buy some of the camels they have for sale."

Sel beamed. "Real camels? They honestly exist?"

I bit back a laugh at his excitement, feeling older and far more jaded. I'd read about camels in a book before, so I'd known they were real, but never really planned or cared to see them.

Gwen looked uncertain and I guessed it was because of the wolves.

I grimaced as I looked at Nyalla. "Will we be okay taking camels with our furry friends? I know horses aren't fond of wolves."

Nyalla brushed my concern aside. "Camels are the most stubborn, difficult animals I've ever encountered, but they don't frighten easily. So long as you don't expect the camels to allow wolves to ride them, I think we'll be fine."

At the image that created, I was unable to hold back my laughter, and soon the others joined in.

Once we'd quieted, Gwen spoke. "I highly doubt the wolves will be interested. I can either send them on ahead or have them trail behind, whichever you think more suitable."

Nyalla glanced at the wolves, a rare expression of fondness crossing her face. "Either would be fine. But it's likely best if I'm in the lead, since I know where to go. Camels will double our speed as well, so instead of what would have been a two-day trip, if we leave when the sun sets tonight, we should get there shortly after dawn. It will mean a longer distance than usual and I'm warning you in advance, if you're not used to camel travel, you're going to be in more pain than you can possibly imagine."

I grimaced, remembering how sore I'd been the first time I'd ridden a horse. If camel travel was worse, I wasn't sure I'd be able to walk.

"If there aren't any stops, we'll do our best to keep up. Unless you guys want to try to break the trip up into two days?" I tilted my head, raising my eyebrows as I waited for the others to weigh in. As expected, they all shook their heads.

"I'm ready for this trip to be done," Will breathed out.

He hadn't complained as much as usual, which may have had something to do with his fascination with Nyalla, but I knew the trip had been difficult for all of us. Although he was the most fit of all of us and accustomed to training hard, the many, many days of walking were something none of us were used to.

"Me too." Sel proclaimed.

Gwen added a tired bob of her head.

I smiled. "I guess it's unanimous. We want to get to the temple to retrieve the Heart Stone as soon as possible.

Nyalla shrugged. "All right, as long as you're prepared to have the sorest backside, you'll ever experience without falling off a three-story building backwards."

I winced, briefly reconsidering my eagerness before remembering either way we traveled I was going to end up sore. The only difference was when we'd be able to get home and lick our wounds. "The sooner the better."

Nyalla nodded, then waved for us to follow her to a small house perched a few paces from the small pond. It had a thatch roof which seemed unlikely to keep rain out, but that didn't seem to be a concern in the desert from what could determine. It was painted a bright white and a cheery contrast to the never-ending sea of beige sand around it.

When Nyalla knocked on the door, an old couple greeted us.

They seemed happy to see us, although I couldn't understand a word they were saying as Nyalla answered them.

Once they were finished, Nyalla nodded and turned to translate. "They are the custodians of the oasis. They bid us a good evening, and they want us to know they are happy to have visitors and can assist us with replenishing our supplies. If you have enough money, they can also sell us three camels."

I frowned. "They don't have any more?"

"Unfortunately, not. Normally a caravan comes by once every handful of days, but we've apparently arrived just after the last one and they didn't have money to purchase more." She leaned closer, dropping her voice. "If I didn't already have a relationship with them, they would only sell us two. They will be stuck here until the next caravan arrives if we take all three."

I looked at the elderly couple, their open faces watching us curiously, similar gap-toothed smiles. They looked endearingly innocent, and the thought of taking the last of their animals felt horribly wrong.

"Nyalla, we can't take all the camels. Could we make do with two? How much weight can a camel carry?"

Nyalla looked at me dubiously and I bristled as she seemed to measure me. "I'm not sure, but the heavier the load, the sooner they'll tire out. If we only have two either someone must walk, or one of the camels will have to carry three people. Even three camels is stretching their strength."

I knew she was right. It wouldn't do to buy camels and exhaust them before we reached our goal.

Nyalla put a hand on my shoulder and gave it a reassuring squeeze. "Really, the custodians will be fine. Keep in mind they live here and know the desert far better than we do. As you can see, they clearly are not underfed and have ample water. They seem pretty confident someone's going to be here within the next day or two and I am certain they wouldn't do anything to put their lives in danger."

When I still looked uncertain, Gwen chimed in.

"Look at them. Nyalla is right. They look quite content, comfortable, and completely unworried. People like they appear to be are too practical to give you their property at personal risk, even for a profit. They know the desert too well to be foolish, the same way I know the Low Forests."

Bowing to their logic, but not sure if it was simply because they were saying what I wanted to hear, I finally agreed.

We replenished our supplies, purchasing an extra flask of water each to carry water in case there was none available where we were going. We even had the luxurious opportunity to wash our bodies and clothing.

Because we were in a safer environment, we took the chance of sleeping all at the same time. After all, it was daytime. Wild animals weren't a huge threat and the old couple promised to wake us if a caravan came or we were attacked.

We'd told them we were interested in any visitors, but not that we were possibly being followed. They hadn't asked questions, and we'd been so grateful for sleep we hadn't lingered to chat.

WE SET out the next evening with our spirits high. Even though the landscape was harsh and barren, with the sun setting in glorious shades of oranges and reds, it made the desert look as if it was on fire. If it wasn't so difficult to get here, I wouldn't mind visiting the oasis again for a vacation.

If we made it out alive.

After a few hours however, all thoughts of the stark beauty surrounding me was gone, replaced by self-flagellation as I reconsidered not only the utility but the wisdom of riding camels. It was true, it was faster than traveling on foot had been, but they were smelly, and spit at the slightest provocation.

The wolves gave them a wide berth even without a warning. Swift and the others had taken one look at the camels and waited several steps behind. If it was possible for a wolf to look disgusted, each of them did. It was absolutely no problem keeping the animals apart as neither wanted anything to do with the other. I couldn't say I blamed them.

Initially I'd been excited about the chance to ride with Gwen.

Will had gallantly offered to ride with Sel, allowing Nyalla to go on ahead. I knew he would have much rather ridden with her, but she hadn't objected, which was why our irritable and stinky small convoy was arranged so Gwen and I were in the back, in relative privacy.

"This is far less romantic than I'd hoped," she complained at the exact moment I was regretting agreeing to the camels.

I turned, wrinkling my nose, and smiling as she shifted uncomfortably in the rough, uncushioned saddles the elderly caretakers had strapped on for us—for a price, of course. It was basically a rolled-up leather blanket with a few straps to hold onto. Hardly comfortable, or stable. I had already been forced to grab on to keep myself from falling when the camel shifted too quickly.

"Well, it may not be glamorous or romantic, but I am glad I get to share this with you." I gave her a smile.

The usual tingle of warmth between us had long since departed in the aftermath of the uncomfortable rocking of the camel. It probably didn't help much of my energy was being spent controlling the vague sense of nausea I felt from the way the camels swayed back and forth with each step.

She leaned forward, catching my lips in a light movement. A spark of joy tempered the nausea and discomfort as she leaned back.

"I think we're going to regret this far more than we know," she wiggled her bottom slightly and bared her teeth.

I nodded glumly, turning my head to look at the others. They were a fair distance ahead of us but easily visible across the flat land, so I turned back and touched my tongue to my lips.

Giving her a mischievous look, I awkwardly maneuvered myself to lean into her. My legs and most of my trunk still faced forward as I wrapped my arms around her and punished her light and teasing kiss with one that was intense, and hot enough so when we pulled away, we were both short of breath. Smiling with satisfaction at her flushed face I leaned back to a more comfortable position.

"There, did that help take your mind off some of your discomfort?" I was uncomfortably warm now, even though it was a cool night.

She nodded mutely, biting her bottom lip as she looked at me intently before finally answering. "I can't wait for this trip to be over. I'd love to have a nice, warm bed and hot bath."

I swallowed hard at the images that came to mind when her eyelids drooped lazily and leaned back for another kiss. Of course, it was the exact moment the camel shifted. Losing my balance, I gripped her thighs and righted myself, heart pounding from exhilaration and fear.

Our eyes met, wide and full of desire and in unison, we burst into laughter.

"I agree. I want to be alone with you in a quiet place, preferably one which doesn't move. I think I'm ready to take our relationship to the next level."

She nodded, the stars in the sky pale in comparison to the stars in her eyes. We may have been in the desert, but right then I felt like I was in the most beautiful rain forest in the world.

"I see it!" Sel's excited shouting interrupted us.

I turned, still breathless from our interlude.

There, rising out of the desert like a phoenix, was the temple.

At first, I could almost convince myself it was another set of caves, like the ones we'd slept in the first day. But after only a few seconds it was obvious the building had been specifically placed there for worship at some point in time.

One peak rose over the sand above the rest of the building. The closer we came, the more I could see of the architecture. Even though the color of the sandstone blended with the desert around it, as though deliberate hands had constructed it. I turned to smile at Gwen once more and turned to face the temple.

Would we find what we were looking for? And what else would we find inside?

OUR DISMOUNT from the camels proved awkward, painful, and hilarious. I managed to keep myself from falling by half-sliding, half jumping. To my surprise and amusement, Will was the one who landed face first in the sand. It may have had something to do with Sel attempting to get off the camel at the same time, but it provided a welcome distraction from the feeling someone had decided to sever all the muscles in my inner thighs. It was the worst pain I could remember, and the first few steps felt as if somebody was trying to make sure I was unable to run ever again.

We hobbled toward the half-buried entrance, the large stone blocks which made up the walls and the archway worn by the sand and time, yet still fitting perfectly together. It looked as if someone had scooped out an area near the door, and to my surprise, it stood wide open. I exchanged cautious looks with the others as Nyalla began to venture inside.

Putting a hand out, I stopped her. "If the temple is anything like other places housing objects of immense value, this door should have been locked. There should be traps, ways to keep out the unworthy." I shook my head and narrowed my eyes as I looked around the empty entryway. "I think someone's been here. Look."

The others followed my finger to the footprints visible just inside the doorway. With the light from Will's torch, I looked at the walls and ceiling, noting darts lying nearby on the ground. My heart sank.

"What do you think that means?" Will pointed to the opposite end of the room, where another door hung ajar, a piece of wood appearing to be keeping it open.

"I think it means we're too late." Gwen's voice was resigned, and she patted my shoulder. Nyalla looked furious. "How is this possible? No one passed us."

I shook my head, hardly registering her uncharacteristic anger as I cautiously moved through the room to the other door, sliding between the makeshift lever and the door.

The inner sanctum was right there, with a pedestal directly beneath the sunlight. The sun was just rising, so it wasn't brightly lit, but I knew at midday the sun would shine directly onto the empty pedestal beneath it.

CHAPTER 19

I waved a hand at the pedestal, then allowed it to slap against my thigh. "Well, that answers that question."

I glared at the empty spot for moment before shifting my gaze to the rest of the room. Gwen looked as upset as I felt, and Will and Sel appeared disappointed. I allowed myself a glance at Nyalla, but her initial fury had given way to a speculative look.

"I can't believe it!" I growled at the room, clenching my fists, and banging them on the sides of my legs hard enough I could feel it. "This has been a complete waste of time. It's gone. Someone beat us here."

Gwen looked at me, a commiserating expression on her face, but I was having none of it. Everything we'd gone through—being kidnapped, thrown into a dungeon, escaping, days of walking in the desert. All a complete waste.

"We had no proof it was going to be here in the first place," Will said, keeping his voice mild.

I turned to him with a snarl. "Of course, we did! It was all there in the books. Granted, the landscape looks different now, but it was supposed to be here!"

My frustration echoed loudly through the chamber,

increased by the fact none of my friends appeared to understand the depth of my emotion. I'd reached the end of the journey where the prize was supposed to be waiting, and instead had been rewarded with nothing. This wasn't how it was supposed to be. Why would the Library send us here for nothing?

"Look," he gestured around the room. "There's more here than just the stone, which I assume was supposed to be on the pedestal? Look at the rest of the room."

In my singled-minded focus, he'd noticed what I hadn't. He was right. Although less stocked than the Library by far, the room had its own variety of books, parchments, and scrolls. None of which appeared to have the Heart Stone, unfortunately.

"Yeah, that's great. But if scavengers beat us here and took the stone, all of this is useless. There's no way to find out where the stone went by reading anything here."

Even as frustration threatened to burn me up from inside, curiosity stirred in my soul. I ruthlessly tried to shut it down. I knew I sounded like a spoilt child to the others present, but my complaint was valid.

The Library wanted me to find the Heart Stone, which meant at best these books were a distraction, and at worst, they may keep me from finding what I needed.

"True, they won't tell you where the stone is now. But I bet something in here could still be useful." He smiled brightly.

His words were irritating, but I could tell he was trying to lighten my mood. Sadly, it wasn't helping. I sat down on the floor knees splayed as I rested my head on my palms. The ground beneath my feet had a brown stain which looked suspiciously like blood.

Far too much for it to have been a minor injury.

Sadness for others who had lost their lives looking for the stone suddenly filled me with a wave of hopeless despair. I had no idea what to do next.

A gentle hand patted my shoulder and I looked up, expecting Gwen. I blinked when I saw Nyalla's smooth expression.

"I can see you're upset," she began.

I snorted at the obviousness of her statement, but she ignored my rudeness.

"It's easy to see you have trust issues, but I'm hopeful we can find the stone. I know the people of this desert and I know this land. We would've been here days earlier had I realized this is where you meant to go."

"Maybe we would've beat whoever took it," Will muttered, earning another glare from me. He pressed his lips together tightly and fell silent.

Nyalla shot him a half-smile before crouching next to me. "I don't think you're right, based on the amount of dust here."

Nyalla gestured to the area around the pedestal. She was right. Whoever had taken the Heart Stone had taken it long ago, months, or even longer, well before I'd had any sign from the Library I needed to search for it. Nyalla's casual observation made me feel far better than any of Will's comments had so far.

"You're right," I agreed, giving her a tentative smile. "I was so upset to not see the stone I didn't realize the sand and dust is too thick for someone to have beaten us by only days. Although it doesn't help us find it, it does make me feel a little better about our journey not being a waste."

Nyalla nodded, accepting the unspoken apology. "Exactly. Which means someone was looking for the stone prior to the start of your travels." She paused, looking at me intently. "I know you don't trust me, but I promise I can help you find the stone. You just have to believe me. Give me a chance."

I looked into her earnest face, wondering again why I was having so much trouble with her. Even as the key pulsed gently, reminding me of its cautious presence, I couldn't think of a single occasion where she had done anything to harm us.

Hadn't she fed us, kept us safe, and kept us from getting lost? She'd even found camels for the trip, which granted, could fall into either the harm or help category.

It was a tough choice. The guys had fallen under her spell, if they weren't madly in love with her. Even Gwen had softened. Except for the one night where Nyalla had referred to herself as Y'serra, I had nothing tangible to base my worries on.

Not to mention we still had no better way to find the stone.

"I do trust you, Nyalla. It's just, well, I'm not used to telling people what I'm thinking. Even my friends." I shrugged, giving her an apologetic look as I caught nods of agreement from the guys.

Gwen looked thoughtful but didn't agree or disagree.

Nyalla opened her eyes wide, hope radiating out of her. "Does that mean you'll trust me from now on? I need to know everything you do if we hope to find the stone. I may know the people and the land here, but you're the one with the information. If you think something might be important to help find its location, you'll have to let me know from now on. Can you promise me you'll keep me updated?"

I took a deep breath. The key pulsed and even as I outwardly promised to Nyalla I would trust her, I promised the key I would tell her as little as possible to make sure the Heart Stone didn't fall into the wrong hands.

Whether or not those hands were Nyalla's, I had no idea. The key calmed slightly but didn't return to the same cool surface it normally possessed.

I could feel it was waiting, still cautious, and although I smiled for the sake of the others, I knew there was no way I'd ever trust Nyalla fully. Not so long as I remembered her connection to Y'serra.

"Great!" Her face broke into a triumphant smile.

Will and Sel looked similarly excited, but Gwen maintained the thoughtful, intent expression she'd worn earlier.

"So now what?" I stood, brushing the dirt off my pants.

As everyone turned to Nyalla, she looked around the room, then strode across to the wall behind the empty podium. "Here," she pointed at a map I hadn't noticed earlier. "I was hoping to see something like this."

I squinted at it, but it wasn't one I recognized. It hadn't been in the books or papers I'd found on the region.

"How is it helpful?" Gwen moved closer to get a better look.

Nyalla pointed at the lines on the paper. "Even if the landscape has changed, the topography remains mostly the same. Take away the trees and the rivers, and you'll always be left with solid ground underneath."

When she nodded her understanding, Nyalla continued.

"There are several towns where the Oubliee live, and they are all arranged around this temple. Even though many are within an easy day's distance, no one comes here anymore, as nothing of value remains."

When I looked at the books and frowned, Nyalla shook her head.

"Those may be of value to you, or to another scholar or Librarian, but when people live in the desert, things such as books and parchment are useless except for wiping yourself once you've had a bowel movement or to start a fire on a cold night. While it is surprising so many remain, my guess is it was likely too much work for too little reward."

Will pursed his lips. "They probably thought the temple was haunted or cursed. Or more likely, it wasn't worth risking booby-traps just to get enough kindling to last a few hours."

"Exactly. Someone did trip them at some point, likely when the valuables and possibly the Heart Stone were taken."

Although my distrust lingered, everything she said made sense. "Where would you recommend we head from here? Is there any place you can think of which would be more likely to harbor the stone?"

I heard the hope in my voice. Was I was being naïve? Here I was, unable to trust my guide yet still hoping the answers would drop into my lap.

"Not exactly," she shook her head. "I think we should take the camels to the nearest town and rest there before we make plans. With any luck, the scavengers won't have made it to the town we're going. I have some friends who can shelter us there for the day, and if they haven't heard anything, we'll travel by night to the next town."

I looked up at the skylight dubiously. The room was now much brighter. "How far is it? Surely it will be too hot for us to make it all the way there now."

Nyalla followed my gaze. "With the camels? About an hour. Without, usually two or three. If we leave now, I think we can make it before it becomes unbearably hot. I recommend completely covering your faces though, as even the morning sun can burn strong men in minutes."

As I looked around the room, I wasn't sure why we couldn't stay, but it was already becoming uncomfortably warm as the sun moved higher in the sky. The temple may provide partial shelter from the elements, but if it was only an hour to the nearest town it would be best to leave now, especially if we wanted to keep the camels healthy.

"I'm game if you guys are." Will spoke first, while Sel nodded in response.

I looked at Gwen, who inclined her head. Exhaling, I added my agreement. "Okay, I'll trust you. Let's go."

Nyalla clapped her hands, taking on a brisk air. "Excellent! If there's anything you want, take it now. It will likely go the way of whatever else was in the rooms we passed through. Otherwise, get back to the camels. This will be a most uncomfortable trip."

We carefully searched the room but found nothing of value as expected. disappointed at coming all this way for nothing, I mounted the camel with more difficulty than at the oasis due to protesting muscles.

As the camels plodded on and the temple faded into the desert behind us, I peered through the narrow slits in my scarf which allowed me to see. Even though it was nearly suffocating me, I was thankful for the thick material.

In moments, the temple was swallowed by the desert and I turned to face what lay ahead.

What was I was getting us into by trusting Nyalla with our lives? Would I live long enough to find out?

CHAPTER 20

Nyalla had been accurate at estimating the time it would take, but when we arrived at the first town, I swiftly realized town meant a small outpost.

There couldn't have been more than forty houses in front of us, made from the same material the ones in the scavenger's village had been. The size of the community made sense when I looked at the sparse housing closely nestled together near a rocky outcropping with a tiny creek. The area could probably only support a few families at a time.

When Nyalla caught my concern, she chuckled. "Don't worry, people here have adapted to their conditions. Each of the towns I know of are at most a few hours walk apart. Close enough to trade and marry outside of immediate families, but far enough they don't drain place the other group's subsistence level industries."

"What kind of things do they trade?" Gwen was looking at the houses with interest. I could tell she was intrigued by a life-style so different from hers in the forest. I had always thought of her as a loner and couldn't picture her living so close to anyone other than her wolves, which gave my heart a strange twinge of pain.

"It depends on the location. Some of the villages mine coal, which can be burnt for heat and light, others on the river, such as this one harvest fish, and a few have hillside terraces which have been painstakingly cultivated for growing food. Each has developed a niche, but they are all interdependent."

I bit my lip, considering her words. "So, does you think that because they are so interdependent the Heart Stone may have made its way along the trading route?"

She smiled, pleased at my guess. "Exactly my suspicions. The man I know here, in what they call Johnstown, is someone who'd know if anything out of the ordinary has come through the market lately." She leaned over, lowering her voice. "Legal and illegal, if you know what I mean."

I nodded my head but had no idea what she meant. I looked at Will, who raised and lowered his eyebrows quickly a few times. I'd have to ask him what kind of things went on in an illegal market when we weren't in such an unsecured area.

Nyalla showed us where to tie up the camels, and once they were secure, knocked on a small hut beside the hitching post.

"I'm coming, I'm coming! Don't you know it's rude to wake someone up?" The voice was grumpy and gruff, but the person who opened the door was human and friendly looking. His eyes had been drawn together in a frown which quickly changed to a smile, complete with twinkling eyes and a dimple in his left cheek.

"Nyalla! I didn't know you were coming through here! Why didn't you tell us?"

"I didn't know I was, John, or I would have. Besides, you know I would've reached here prior to any word of my trip."

"True. So, how long are you staying this time?" He opened the door wide and ushered us in. He barely seemed to register the fact we were strangers. It seemed as if any friend of Nyalla's was a friend of his.

"Any relation to the John this town is named after?" Will tilted his head as he looked at the other man.

John burst out in a belly laugh so hard it caused tears to spring to his eyes and he wiped them as he shut the door behind us. The temperature dropped a good five to ten degrees, a pleasant change from the heat I felt was baking my thick robes into my skin.

I wasn't sure what kind of system allowed the place to be so pleasantly cool, until I saw several small windows higher up.

Three were arranged at ninety-degree angles on one wall, and several smaller ones were peppered across each of the other walls of the hut. I marveled at the ingenuity as the cross-breeze cooled me.

Each of the windows also possessed a screen which, when set at an angle, blocked the harsh sand from entering even while allowing the breeze to cool the heat from the sun. What did they do at nighttime to keep it from getting too cold? I was distracted from my thoughts when I caught the conversation between Nyalla and John.

"Heart Stone, you say?"

I winced. I hadn't realized the obvious problem with asking around about the location of the Heart Stone—how many people would find out about it. It was a dilemma I didn't see any way out of though, so I was grateful Nyalla kept the question as vague as possible.

"Yes, probably would have come through in the last few months. Anything unusual lately?"

John thought for a moment, then shook his head. "Sorry, nothing out of the ordinary has been traded to my knowledge. Maybe head to Billstown. He might know something."

Nyalla exhaled, covering her disappointment with another bright smile. "Thanks John. Would it be possible to resupply and rest here until dusk? We'll move along as soon as it cools down."

"Absolutely. How about I rustle up some grub and you tell me what you need for your pack. You have camels?" Nyalla nodded and John matter-of-factly added, "we best put them inside the stables for now. It's hot, even for a camel."

"Thanks. I was hoping you'd be able to tell us where the stone is, but this helps just as much. How far to Billstown from here?"

John thought for minute, holding out a hand and moving it in a seesaw motion. "About two or three hours, give or take. Seeing as how you've got camels, likely only two. Unless they're old camels."

Nyalla shook her head. "No, they're fairly good. All right. Once we've rested, we'll head to Billstown. Thanks again for taking us in."

John nodded and his face became serious. "You'd best be careful. I've been hearing talk lately about ur'gel. Only last night we heard tell of an attack in Rosetown. Wasn't good. Only a couple handfuls of people made it out. Some of them made it here, some of them best I understood, headed for Billstown. Seems like we're seeing a lot more of them things lately."

I gulped, wondering what kind of ur'gel could take on an entire village. Either enormous numbers, such as the ones who'd attacked us in the Low Forest, or perhaps the bigger ones I'd read about in the books, the ones I'd had nightmares about after our last encounter.

"Thanks for the warning, John. We'll be careful."

Nyalla rested a hand on John's beefy forearm and he patted it with his other hand.

Will cleared his throat and stepped forward. "I don't suppose as part of your supplies you'd have any extra weapons to sell?"

John narrowed his eyes, looking down at Will and his wirier form with a shrewd expression. "Might. What are you looking for, youngster?"

He shrugged. "We have some short swords, but if you had something a little better for fighting larger opponents, I'd appreciate it. It's just us, but we only have three short swords to go around."

John wrinkled his nose, giving Gwen and I a skeptical once over before looking at Sel and raising an eyebrow. "I'll see what I can find. Might be hard for anybody here to have the strength to use a bigger weapon effectively."

Sel narrowed his eyes and I knew he felt as if his honor was being called into question, but he wisely held his tongue.

"I would be grateful. Perhaps you could bring a variety?" I gave him as winning a smile as I could muster. "We may not be strong, but surely if we test a few out we might find something we can handle."

John's forehead creased. "I'll see what I can do. For now, though, you guys have a seat. I put away what was left of supper last night. Lucky for you, I made enough for seconds and thirds, so there should be enough for everybody to have a portion. While you eat, I'll ask around town and see what I can rustle up for supplies."

JOHN PROVED as good as his word. Within minutes, full bowls of a decent smelling stew were placed in front of us with thick hunks of a coarse bread. While the bread wasn't up to the quality Will's mother or Marthe had shared with us in Sunglen and Midland, it was filling and tasty.

We ate quickly over light conversation, mostly filled with Nyalla and John reminiscing about mutual acquaintances. Once we'd finished eating, Nyalla shooed John out.

Gwen and I helped her tidy while the guys arranged the sleeping quarters he'd shown us prior to leaving.

When he returned, his small hut was tidy, and our sleeping mats were ready. Based on Nyalla's happy expression, his procurements were exactly what she'd hoped for and she quickly repacked our bags with food and water. He saved the weapons for last and we followed him outside to find an arrangement of about ten different swords and knives leaning against the wall.

Will immediately went for the largest one. I kept my mouth shut but was impressed with how easily he wielded it. Apparently, John was as well, because his attitude toward him improved dramatically. Sel stuck with a thinner version almost the same length, while Gwen and I picked long daggers the size of my forearm. We wouldn't be able to keep a large ur'gel at bay for long, but I knew I'd topple over trying to swing anything larger.

Once restored and replenished, we fell into a deep sleep.

Although I'd wanted to stand guard the way we'd done most days, the others had argued because we were in a safe house there was no need. Reluctantly I caved, hoping the key around my neck which pulsed gently from time to time would warn me if any danger approached. Still uncertain about the path ahead, I fell into a deep, dreamless sleep.

We left as the sun set. Our camels were fresh and easily made it to Billstown within the two hours John had estimated.

Bill proved to be every bit as friendly as John but knew just as little about the stone and directed us toward Gagetown, promising if we found Gage, he may know more.

We jumped back on the camels and headed down the dusty path which interlocked the villages of the Oubliee. Each town had a slightly different terrain and niche as Nyalla had pointed out earlier and when I considered the desolate region, I found it was an ingenious system for maximizing everyone's independence and interdependence.

When we arrived in Gagetown, we stayed an even shorter length of time. It was the first time I'd seen her look uncertain, even afraid. She had us stay on the camels as she rushed to another small hut and knocked on the door.

She spoke with the man who answered too low for me to hear, then shook her head. Giving him a quick hug and a kiss on both cheeks, she ran back and jumped on the camel, kicking it to get it moving.

At the questioning looks on our faces, she shook her head. "We can talk later. We need to move. Ur'gel are on the way. If we stay, we'll regret it."

We didn't argue, but it was clear something had changed since we'd begun wandering the desert. It now felt imperative that if we were going to stop, the town needed to be a fortified location. We didn't question her decisions, instead heading to the next stop she had on her list—Jamestown.

There, the same pattern replayed itself. We'd hardly entered the town when Nyalla got a look on her face. She led us to a house where she chatted briefly with someone, this time a woman, and without stopping, once again led us out of town.

I waited until we were alone and away from the small community to question her. "What's going on? Did you even ask her about the stone?"

Nyalla looked at me, her mouth set in a grim line. "I did. But more ur'gel are on the way, and we need to get out of here. Each time we stop I'm asking the person who would know the most about movement in and out of their territory. If they don't know, they pass me on to the next person."

"So, where's the next stop?"

To my surprise, it was Sel who spoke up. He sat on the camel with Will, both alert and looking around for danger.

I couldn't see any benefit to her lying over this and believed her when she told us ur'gel were on the way. After leaving Gagetown, she'd also shared news of other ur'gel attacks in neighboring villages, which was partly why we were headed back toward the mountain range of the Dragon Dominion.

"We're heading to a scavenger's stronghold. Gemma was speaking with one of the local black-market merchants earlier this week and believes they may know something."

I winced. "Is it safe to be going back to the same place we escaped?"

Nyalla bit the inside of her cheek. "Safety is an illusion. With ur'gel swarming the Northwestern Lands, I'm not sure anywhere is safe. Besides, this town isn't the same place we left. That is Jaydraberg."

I nodded. "Of course. Tell me, is there any place in the desert not named after a person?"

Even under the circumstances, Nyalla smiled at my irritation. "It's a straightforward way to keep track of who lives where. Every clustering of houses or towns is named for the head of a clan group in charge. Everyone knows who is in power, and it helps when it comes to arranging marriages."

Gwen's eyebrows raised. "How exactly does that work?"

Nyalla tilted her head, pointing in the direction of the town we'd just left. "If people know where you came from, they also know who your family is. With tribes like this, if you were to marry locally, the children become sick and weak after only a generation or two. By marrying people from neighboring villages or better, villages which are farther away, it keeps the blood lines strong. Foreigners are usually viewed with suspicion at first, but if they prove to be attractive and useful, they are valuable commodities."

I saw the look passing between the guys. For the first time it crossed my mind there may have been another reason for a kidnapping us above just stealing our valuables. "Do you mean to say part of the reason we were kidnapped is because we may..."

"Have made good slaves?" Will interjected.

My eyes widened and I shook my head. "I was going to say breeding partners, but I would pretty much have to be a slave to go for that." I wrinkled my nose at the distasteful idea.

Nyalla shot me a commiserating look. "Slave or bride. Either way, it was a possibility. May still be, in fact." She included us all with a wry smile, adding, "Although running away may not have been in their intentions for you, it could actually raise your value in their eyes."

Gwen choked, then quickly coughed to hide her reaction. She regained control finally, managing to ask, "You mean breaking out of prison was a good thing?"

"With these people, sometimes. It shows spirit, grit, and determination, if not necessarily wisdom. Those traits are prized here, where the land can quickly wear down the weak of heart and spine, and the strong have more children. Besides, as much as I hate to admit it, your wolves would be enough to attract a high price, even if they didn't like you."

I felt her shocked recoil behind me on the camel and had to stifle a laugh. I think it was the first time anyone had ever considered her and the wolves a valuable package.

"Why do they like the wolves so much?" Sel asked.

I waited for Nyalla to respond, envying her easy grace on the camel. Every step mine took made me lurch from side to side, but she appeared to be sitting on nothing more inconvenient than a swinging chair.

"The wolves are valuable because they not only provide for themselves, but with the right master or mistress, they have the potential to feed many mouths in a village. Wolves are worth double what a human is. Even the stray dogs you've seen wandering the streets are valuable friends. And they have no special qualities other than being able to provide for themselves."

"Huh."

Everyone fell silent as we carried on to the next town. But just before arriving, Nyalla looked startled and turned, her eyes wide. "Change of plans. We need to go to Jaydraberg. Right now."

I wanted to argue, but the fear in her eyes outweighed any objection I could make. What made it worse was the fact we could see the next village only a few minutes off in the distance and I was certain Jaydraberg would add at least an hour to our journey, if not longer.

As we changed directions, the night wind brought the reason for our abrupt change of direction into perspective.

The clash of metal rang in the night, shattering the silence as screams rang out.

I knew the others had heard the same thing as we nudged our camels to follow Nyalla at a faster clip.

None of us were eager to return to Jaydraberg, but we'd also never been this close to becoming part of one of the ur'gel attacks which made the decision easier.

IT WAS STILL DARK when we arrived at the high walled town. In comparison to the others we'd been through over the last few nights, it was easy now to see why this would be considered the capital or most important city. Few of the other towns had been walled, and none had approached the size of this one. While it hadn't seemed like much the first time we'd been there, I could now see it for the central trading hub it was.

We entered with as much stealth as we could, through the same hidden doorway into Nyalla's house from which we'd exited, leaving the camels outside. Once we were secure within the house, Nyalla led them around to the main entrance. We waited, silent and still in shock at the night's adventure. While we may have gotten used to the desert wind and sand, hearing an ur'gel attack from up close but not attempting to help sat uncomfortably in my heart and mind.

"I can't believe we just left them." Gwen spoke softly into the quiet room, voicing my thoughts aloud.

I moved closer to where she sat on the floor, laying my head on her shoulder. "I know. It didn't feel right to me either, but what were we going to do to protect an entire town if they couldn't do better themselves?"

Will nodded, his face barely visible in the dim light. "Exactly. I'm not sure if you've noticed, but the Oubliee are far tougher, not to mention more skilled at fighting than any of us."

He paused and even in the dark I saw a smirk across his face. "Well, except for myself course."

I rolled my eyes but felt a little better. He was right, after all. Not to mention the fact even had we been properly outfitted for battle and knew how to fight, we needed to retrieve the stone before chance losing our lives against ur'gel we had sought out.

Maybe I was trying to soothe my conscience, but it seemed to me at that moment, the key pulsed with faint warmth. Calm filled me.

Nyalla returned a moment later, unwrapping her scarf with a pleased expression on her face.

"What happened to the camels?" Sel asked, trying to peer through the narrow window next to the door, as if looking for them outside.

"I sold them to a friend. I gave him a good deal in exchange for some information. It turns out he may know someone who knows where the stone went. We need to leave now though, before daylight. It'll be a lot easier to remain unseen in the dark."

We nodded, leaving everything behind except for my satchel and the weapons we'd managed to retrieve and purchase. Although we were hoping it didn't come down to it, none of us felt safe wandering through town unprotected.

After making sure our protective disguises of scarves and long cotton robes were intact, I followed Nyalla, my hand absently resting over the key on my chest. It was warm, but not in the way I was beginning to associate with imminent danger. I tried to shove my concerns down. Just before we turned the next corner, the key suddenly became so hot I pulled my hand off with a small gasp and looked down. But it was too late.

A soldier stood there, almost an entire head and shoulders larger than Will, brandishing a weapon which made his look like a bread knife in comparison.

"Sisters take me," Nyalla muttered, confirming what the key had warned me. Apparently, he wasn't a friend of hers. She looked at us grimly. "I'm sorry, but this appears to the end of the line for us."

If I'd harbored any hope of overpowering the gargantuan guard, when he was joined by three others I exhaled slowly. It appeared we'd be making another trip to the castle. The only question was; would it be directly to the prison, or would we have a chance to speak with Jaydra and perhaps this time, achieve a better outcome?

INITIALLY IT SEEMED we were destined for lock up, but when the guards surrounding us led us back to the same receiving area to which we'd spoken with the Sovran, I realized they hadn't removed our weapons. Strange, maybe they didn't know we had any? Or perhaps they wanted us to use them to give them an excuse to could kill us. Whatever the reason, I wasn't about to draw attention to them myself.

I knelt where the guard had thrown me and looked around the room. The only difference from our last visit was the room was empty. Other than the guards, we were the only one's present.

One of the guards left while the others took up positions at the front of the room and beside the doorway. The room was lit with torches which gave off a soothing orange glow. It would have been a peaceful scene, if the rapid beat of my heart hadn't echoed in my ears.

The ominous sound of a door creaking caused us all to turn our heads. To my surprise, the guard returned, holding the door as Jaydra glided into the room.

She was every bit as fiercely elegant as I recalled, only this time her hair was down and trailed almost to the floor. I hadn't realized her scarf hid so much hair and although it made her look strangely more approachable, it also made her look more goddess-like and untouchable.

Jaydra gave us a wide berth as she walked around us to sit in her chair, moving her long dress to the side. It was a beautiful dark blue, highlighting her eyes and tanned skin as much as her previous white raider outfit had. Her face wore a mixture of irritation and intrigue.

"My guards have informed me not only did you escape from the prison somehow, but you also managed to get past the walls of the town. The fact you are standing before me means you have also survived the desert, and for some odd reason, had the nerve to come back." She shook her head, clearly marveling at our boldness.

When she put it like that, it *was* audacious, and I realized just how badass we were. It gave me the strength to stand up. I moved cautiously, watching the guards, and expecting to be thrown back on the floor any moment. When they didn't move, I bowed and addressed the Sovran.

"We wouldn't have bothered you again Sovran, only we are in a most important search for the Heart Stone."

I lifted my head, looking directly into her eyes. She tilted her head to the side with interest, waving for me to go on instead of cutting me off the way she had the last time. I rushed on in case she changed her mind.

"Everything I'd read told me the Heart Stone was found in the temple in the Desert of Souls, which the old writings refer to as Mahimānbita Sūrya. But when we got there after several days of uncomfortable travel—" I stopped, looking down at Nyalla.

I thought I'd heard something, but she was kneeling and looking at the floor along with the others. I looked at Jaydra again and shook my head.

"When we arrived, the stone was gone. It had clearly been gone a several weeks, if not longer. The dust had been disturbed and the traps had been set off, but sand had reaccumulated and there were no footprints. As I'm sure you can understand, it was quite frustrating. We left the temple and traveled through the desert, hoping to find word of its current location." I shrugged. "But no one had any information. The last place we were going to ask was under attack by ur'gel, so we changed course and headed back here."

Jaydra laughed, and I recoiled at the out of place humor. Surely, I hadn't said anything funny?

"Oh, you foolish elf." She gave me a patronizing smile. "Beru took the stone when he came through. I could have saved you time, had I listened to your ramblings more closely. But before you ask, I have no idea where he took it. Now, you clearly found our hospitality lacking last time, but please allow my guards to take you to holding. You may rest until I decide what to do with you."

She yawned, and with a dismissive flick of her wrist, the guards converged upon us. As their implacable faces loomed closer, I swallowed hard, certain we were going back to the same cage we'd escaped from earlier.

The problem was this time, our rescuer was with us.

CHAPTER 21

"This is such a pile of disgusting dog dung."

I crossed my arms and glared at the door to our prison. Sure, Jaydra had kindly called it a holding area, not a prison, and it was somewhat nicer than our last accommodations had been, but that wasn't saying much.

It was larger, and without bars. It also had places for everyone to sit, which was a pleasant change. It even had pillows. In fact, even though my mood had become terribly sour since we'd been led to our waiting area, I could grudgingly admit it would not have looked out of place as a place to receive guests at Cliff Castle.

Will sat on one of the overstuffed couches and lay back, groaning a little. From the way he was rolling back and forth on the surface I suspected his sound was one of pleasure, which was confirmed immediately when he yawned, "*Ah*, this is nice."

He opened his eyes and gestured for us to join him. "Seriously, guys. This is the softest thing I've laid on in forever. Definitely since before we hitched our ride on the airship."

Gwen took my hand and gently led me over to a couch opposite him. Once I was seated, she patted my knee. "I know you're frustrated, Rhin. I'm frustrated too. It feels like we're missing everything, but it's only by a single step."

I exhaled, visualizing the weight of my frustration leaving my body as I did so. Will was right. This was comfortable. I sank into the couch and leaned back, resting my head against one of the cushions.

"Part of what's bothering me is being stuck in here until Jaydra decides what to do with us, but I'm also confused about something." I turned my head. "Will I ever be able to find it? Is it already too late?"

She shook her head, furrowing her brow as she regarded me. "I don't understand. Why would it be too late?"

I leaned forward, directing my words to everyone. "Because. Beru was Onen Suun's first Lieutenant. If he had the Heart Stone, maybe it never made it back to the pedestal in the first place." I looked at Nyalla.

"What do you mean?"

I waved a hand in the air, more of my frustration leaking out in the motion. "If he found it before he got locked up in the prison, he could have already given it to Dag'draath. In which case there's no way I'm ever going to get it back, no matter if I'm supposed to, according to the Library."

I pulled my hand away, rubbing my temples in futile to ease some of the headache the situation had caused.

"That doesn't make sense. If he had the Heart Stone in the prison, why would Jaydra know about it? Wouldn't he have used it already?"

I dropped my hands from my head. She had a point. "You're right. Maybe Jaydra was saying he came by recently because he had got it two-hundred and fifty years ago and hid it before he was trapped."

Now Nyalla looked excited. "Which means when he came back, he went and got it from where he'd hidden it then, which may not have been from the temple your book told you it was."

"Exactly!" I jumped to my feet and began to pace. "So, it

may not have even been where we thought when he was imprisoned, but if he came back this way it must have been in the desert. The question is—"

"Where would he be taking it now?" Sel spoke up. He had sat was next to Will and his slender face was thoughtful.

"And there lies the problem," I agreed. The impossibility of the situation struck me afresh. "The land in this area has changed immeasurably in the last two hundred years. We found the temple, but it clearly isn't what it was, and the desert wasn't even there when my books were written."

She agreed. "For all we know he might've hidden the stone in a tree."

Will looked unperturbed. When I frowned at him, he shrugged. "What? Look, I have faith in you, Rhin. If anyone can figure this out it's going to be you. But in the meantime, I'm tired, I'm dirty, and this couch is so comfortable I could fall asleep right now. Why don't we use this opportunity to rest? After all, with the guards outside and the one reason we were able to escape last time inside with us, it's not as if we have many options."

I rubbed my forehead again, knowing he was right. As much as I wanted to disagree with him, I couldn't. "Sure, why not?"

I allowed Gwen to draw me down onto the couch. It seemed as if regardless of what happened next, we probably had plenty of time for a nap. But just when I had allowed myself to get comfortable, the thoughts playing in my head coalesced. For some reason, the Library still wanted me to get the Heart Stone even after it had been reclaimed by Beru.

Was I going to have to fight him? The tablets in the Suun Room had shown me the truth about what had happened. Beru was innocent. If he wasn't evil though, why did the Library want me to take the stone? And if he was on the side of darkness, it was extremely unlikely I'd be able to retrieve it.

I couldn't help but think about the way I'd fought with the

slaver, with a skill and technique impossible to have been my own. The more I considered the situation, the more I felt as if the Library had gifted me with a some of Beru's legendary fighting prowess. So how would I defeat him?

With those thoughts hanging heavy over me, my rest was far from peaceful as my friends slept deeply around me.

CHAPTER 22

After an uneasy sleep spent tossing and turning on the most comfortable surface I'd slept on since leaving my own bed, I was startled awake by the sound of the door opening.

The heavy booted feet of one of the guards stopped just inside the door.

I sat up, wiping the side of my mouth and grimaced as I noticed a small patch of drool on Gwen's shoulder. Hopefully, she wouldn't notice.

Will and Sel bolted upright at the same time I did.

Nyalla and Gwen moved more slowly.

Once the guard was certain he had our attention, he nodded toward the door. "The Sovran will see you now." His tone was clipped and didn't invite further discussion.

We stood, scooping up our belongings and taking them with us.

I still wasn't sure why they had allowed us to keep our weapons, unless it was because they no longer thought we were much of a threat. Or did it mean we weren't prisoners?

My apprehension mounted as we entered the throne room again. From the angle the sun fell through the window, it was afternoon at the latest, a fact which caused my stomach to rumble almost on cue. It had been hours since we'd eaten, but even though we'd been summoned earlier then I had expected, I didn't hold much hope for food anytime soon.

Once again, we knelt on the floor a safe distance from the Sovran's chair. Guards flanked her, and although the room was not as empty as it had been earlier, neither was it as full as it had been the first day we'd arrived. From the others present, it looked as if she had cleared the room of all but her most important and trusted advisors. No supplicants requiring favors or payments were in evidence, and those present crowded closely behind her.

My head jerked at the sound of the door grinding to a close and I watched as two guards took up positions in front. We were outnumbered and even if we had weapons this time, I knew we had no chance at getting away unless it was through her direct order.

I turned to Jaydra, bowing my head for a long moment before looking up respectfully. She'd changed again, this time into a bronze colored tunic and loose flowing pants which gathered tightly at the ankles. Her hair was up, which was a pity, as it truly was her best feature. But most surprisingly, her expression was one of amusement.

"After a long discussion with my advisors," she began, waving to either side of her chair to where the other men and women stood in deferential postures. Several bobbed their heads at her regard as she looked at me. "I have decided to let you go."

I blinked, unable to do more as I tried to process her words. But as she continued speaking, I realized why she appeared to find the situation humorous.

"It has come to my attention after much debate with my advisors that Beru and his companion were headed toward the Western March." She smiled, but I saw no kindness in it.

"The Western March?" I was dumbfounded.

It wasn't just far, no, it was on the other side of another mountain range. The place the Oubliee lived in the Northwestern Lands was flanked by the Dragon Dominion on one side and the mountain range before the Western March. It was where the D'ahvol lived and wasn't a place for the faint of heart. Even if we were better equipped, it would be dangerous to go there.

Jaydra laughed, a cold, bell-like peal that echoed in the nearly empty marble room. "Yes, the Western March. When I discovered this, I could not help but see your predicament as entertaining. I expect you would like to be on your way. If you wish to make it there at any time in the next several weeks or months, that is." She smirked again, then as she'd done before, flicked her wrist and turned away.

She'd obviously told us everything she intended to, but it was unclear if she'd done us any favors. As I stood there, unmoving and still bewildered, Jaydra and her advisors filed out. Soon, we were left alone and staring at each other. Most of the guards filed out with her, but the two at the door remained.

Will stood and brushed his knees off. "Well? Shall we?" The others stood as well, hesitating as they looked at the door until he added, "I think it wise to use this as our opportunity to get out before they change their minds."

He kept his eyes on the guards and Gwen exhaled, nodding her head as she came to stand beside me.

She looped her arm through mine. "I agree. Let's go back to Nyalla's and grab the packs. I'm not in a lingering mood."

Sel bit his lip as he looked at Nyalla. "Can we take camels? How far is it to the borders of the Western March?"

She shook her head. "Several days, at least. Yes, we can take camels, although they won't do well in the mountains. I agree with about the necessity of leaving immediately. Even if there are ur'gel out there, we've been given a rare chance to leave. We need to take it." Her eyes narrowed as she cast a glance in the direction Jaydra had exited. "The Sovran is not known for her patience. If we do not act immediately on her command, which this was, make no mistake, she has been known to rescind a gift and replace it with punishment."

I flicked my gaze toward the guards, noticing they were beginning to shift, and I nodded. "Agreed. We'll head to Nyalla's first. It's still daylight though. Is it wise to start traveling now?"

From the grim look on her face, I could tell she wasn't keen on it. But as we had no other option, she just shrugged.

We followed the guards out, and once we were deposited at the entrance to the castle they turned and allowed us to walk away through the market. We weren't being chased this time, so I had a better opportunity to observe the town during a regular day.

The people we encountered were dressed in less coverings than we'd adopted in the desert, but everyone had a scarf and long robes. I imagined the wind could still pick up even with the barrier of the wall and buildings.

It was hard to determine friendliness though. The prickle of eyes on my back didn't let up until we reached Nyalla's home, but I expected nothing less. After all, we were strangers, and from the interested and watchful eyes of the townsfolk, it was probable everyone had heard of our escape and return. By the time we reached her house and gathered our things, I was eager to leave.

We waited as Nyalla returned with camels, but when I noticed they weren't the same as before, I frowned. “Where did these come from?”

She shrugged. "My friend, no longer needing to trade information, was kind enough to provide us with fresh, untraveled ones."

I did my best to keep my lip from pulling back as I examined our new transport dubiously. At least her friend had managed to find us an extra one, but these camels didn't look nearly as young or well as the three we'd had previously.

Nyalla led us down a winding path to the main gates. I realized when she stopped to deliberately speak with the watchman, she was making it obvious our party was leaving. I still didn't trust her, but I couldn't fault her logic.

Once she'd finished speaking with the younger of the two watchmen, she hopped off her camel and offered the reins to Gwen. "I need to go back for something. Continue toward the West. It's a straight path to the mountain pass as we discussed, and I've drawn a rough map for you to use."

She passed me a piece of parchment which I took reflexively. She wasn't joking when she said it was rough, but the way was clear enough. She'd drawn the required changes in topography clearly enough for us to make our way through the mountains. It would be easy enough to follow, even without a guide.

"What are you going back for?" I tried to keep my voice light, but I suspected it was an excuse to leave us. I didn't mind, necessarily, but she'd wanted to leave so badly before it struck me as odd she would take off now.

"There's something I need to do," Nyalla said mysteriously, without volunteering any more information.

"You can't go." Will shook his head, looking at her as if his world was crumbling before him. "We'll never make it through the desert without you."

Nyalla reached over, patting his leg gently, allowing her fingers to caress it fleetingly on their way past. I managed to suppress a shudder of unease, but her touch seemed to do the trick and his sadness gave way to the same adoration I'd noticed over the last few days and weeks.

"Don't worry, you'll be fine. Today will be warm for a few hours, but once night falls, I recommend continuing without sleep. With the camels, you may even be able to reach the pass by morning."

The guys looked disappointed, and even Gwen looked a little sad, but I was relieved. I still didn't trust her even though it looked as if she'd won everyone else over. The key lay calmly against my chest for the first time in days, and I knew at least something else agreed with me.

"Thanks for everything, Nyalla." I reached down to shake her hand.

She clasped mine in return, giving me another one of her mysterious smiles before she nodded and vanished back inside the gates.

I had debated earlier whether I should even try to retrieve this stone, but during my fitful rest in the chamber I'd decided if the Library had set me a task. I needed to complete it, no matter who currently had the stone, and no matter what they were planning on using it for. For all I knew, Beru may even give it to me. And if he didn't, I would cross that bridge when I came to it.

I looked at my friends, fully outfitted with packs and camels, and in possession of all our weapons and belongings. The Oubliee had returned everything they'd taken when we'd been given permission to leave. I was happy to be on our way, but even though Nyalla wasn't coming, my throat tightened with foreboding about the trip that lay ahead.

CHAPTER 23

It was liberating to be on our own again, even with my worry our journey would have further unexpected developments. I couldn't deny my relief Nyalla wasn't with us, even if Will was uncharacteristically quiet as he pined for our mysterious guide.

Sel was his usual quiet self, so it was difficult to see any difference, and Gwen was thoughtful, if not appearing overly upset by Nyalla's disappearance. The wolves, oblivious to any drama between its bipedal counterparts, roamed in lazy loops around us.

It was so nice having the camels. The landscape almost flew by on their backs. It was hot but the breeze from the western mountains came directly toward us. It blew an unpleasant amount of sand into any cracks in our clothing, but at least the snow from the mountaintops kept the sun from being completely sweltering.

Even with the camels traveling at twice the speed we could have made by foot, by the time night fell we were nowhere near the mountains. When a rider appeared on the horizon, we all visibly tensed.

"Who is it?" I squinted, unable to make out the shape. It

was large but misshapen, as if it had several heads and more legs than it should. I was intensely concerned about it being a new type of ur'gel we hadn't crossed paths with before.

"Can't tell from here," Will held a hand up to shade his eyes, a frustrated note in his voice. "Maybe if I had one of Captain Baeley's spyglasses I'd be able to see, but it's a little too far for my eyes to make out."

"Well, whoever, or whatever, it is it seems to be moving fast. Do we push the camels, or wait and see who it is? There's only one of them and four of us, and we have weapons this time." I gnawed on the inside of my lip as I considered the odds.

I didn't like the idea of trying to outrun them. Not only might it be difficult to get to safety in such an open expanse, but we'd also be risking our camels. These ones didn't look as resilient as the previous ones and I knew it would be several more days until we reached the Western March. And we had no idea where Beru had headed after there, so it could be even longer.

"No, I think we should stand our ground. Like you said, there's one of them and four of us. Why don't we find a place which provides some protection from the elements, preferably somewhere we don't have to guard ourselves on all sides."

Will's jaw was tight as he silently tracked the oncoming mystery being.

Sel pointed out a dip in the sand. "I see a small bluff over there to the right. It's not much, but it does block the wind. How do you feel about hiding behind it? Or do you want to keep moving?"

I shook my head. "No. Let's set up there. I'd rather have our weapons out and ready over getting caught with our backs to whoever's approaching."

The others agreed and we readied ourselves for attack. The camels were valuable, but we used them on either side of the bluff to make a small, three-sided fort-type structure. It wasn't much, and it would mean harder traveling if they were injured, but two camels on either side of the bluff made a formidable wall. If anyone was on the attack, better them than us if the situation arose. It would at least slow down an attacker.

"Now, we wait," Gwen slowly tossed her knife from hand to hand.

The wolves were at attention, surrounding her on either side with Swift in front as we waited for the unnamed rider to arrive.

"Wait. Is that..." Sel peered through the darkening sky, his mouth open as his nose wrinkled with the effort.

Will whooped with excitement. "Yes! It's Nyalla!"

My heart sank as the key pulsed gently on my chest again. It had been silent since she'd left. While I could be happy it wasn't an ur'gel, I wasn't thrilled she'd caught up so quickly and she hadn't been abandoning us. The further away from the city we'd gone, the more I had hoped she had left us. But it appeared my hope was in vain.

"That's great, guys," I tried to muster a cheer I didn't feel. No one appeared to notice the difference as both boys beamed.

"I was beginning to worry she wouldn't find us." Will smiled dreamily toward the figure.

As it neared, I could now see a human-shaped figure. What we'd initially taken for several heads turned out to be a camel, as well as the pack on her back. Much less frightening, but no less dangerous in my option.

Given we'd already set up a rough shelter, we waited until she arrived. The camels were bored by now, and had settled down to chew on their cud, drooling and placidly closing their eyes and no longer the barrier we'd hoped for if we were going to be attacked.

When she arrived, both guys leapt to her assistance; Will helping her down from the camel and Sel leading it to the where the others lay to tend to its needs. She'd ridden it fast to catch up, and the camel displayed the effort.

"Phew! I'm glad I caught up. I was worried I'd lost you after the last hill." She looked at me, smiling. "You did great with the map, Rhin. Any problems?"

I shook my head. "Nope. Other than the minor heart attack thinking you were an ur'gel, things have been pretty quiet."

Nyalla nodded, looking back toward Jaydraberg. "I'm hoping we've left them behind. They seem to be attacking all of the desert settlements, but I'm hoping they haven't made it to the Western March yet."

I nodded along, watching as she took in the sight of our rough shelter.

"Are you planning on staying here?" She squinted as she looked around, assessing the area we'd barricaded for ourselves.

"We hadn't expected to," Gwen answered. "But if you were an ur'gel we thought it would be good to be prepped. A little shelter for our backsides, so to speak.

Nyalla pressed her lips together, suppressing a laugh. "Good idea. But now I'm here, do you want to keep moving? You've only gone a half-day's journey. Up to you."

I assessed how I felt. After my restless nap, I felt good to keep traveling if the others did. "I'd like to keep going, at least for a few more hours. How about we have refreshments here?"

"Sounds good to me. I can start a fire and we can cook something or have some of the dried goods in the bag," Gwen offered.

Nyalla shook her head. "No fire. It will draw too much attention. I vote we keep moving as well. Sel, did you give the camel water?"

Sel nodded from where he was rubbing her camel down and she smiled.

"Perfect. Let's have a quick bite to eat then pack up. I think we can reach the mountains around dawn. It'll be a lot safer if we can shelter there."

With everyone in agreement, we ate quickly and traveled

the rest of the night. From time to time, the sound of strange creatures echoed in the dark while birds occasionally swooped, their winds cutting the silence as they swished through the air.

Aside from those unsettling sounds, we remained unbothered by predators and were lucky to avoid spotting any ur'gel. It was shortly after daybreak when the mountains appeared over a large sand dune.

While I was doubtful we'd reach them anytime soon, the camels seemed to have an almost magical ability to travel large tracts of land in a way they made it seem effortless. Well, Nyalla and her camel made it seem effortless.

I, on the other hand, felt every single rock and roll of my camel over the sand and knew I would regret my vote to press on when I attempted to dismount. I'd thought my legs would have toughened slightly by now, but apparently, we hadn't rested long enough for recovery to happen.

"Only another hour from here, I think!" Nyalla turned her head, flashing us a smile.

The key pulsed gently, warning me. Now though, I didn't much care. She was telling me something I desperately wanted to hear and while I didn't trust her, my heart leapt.

This time we built a fire when we stopped.

Gwen let the wolves hunt, so before we slept, we were gifted with a bounty of wild hens from their efforts. After cooking the birds over the fire, we gingerly stretched out on our mats after determining the order of fire watch and I immediately fell into deep and dreamless sleep.

The next few days passed in much the same fashion. The only change was the land around us shifting from sandy to rocky. The path Nyalla was taking us along was relatively easy to traverse but the elevation rose steadily, causing me to feel short of breath even though I was on the back of a camel.

Once we were out of the desert and into the mountain pass, we shifted to sleeping during the night again. The chill of the high mountain snow had tempered the heat and traveling in the dark was more dangerous because of the terrain.

Several days went as we picked our way carefully through the pass. When we finally entered the northern edge of the Low Forest and the mountains gave way to grass and trees, my heart sang at the familiarity. I hadn't been to this part of the Low Forest before, but it still felt like home.

By the time nightfall came on the second day passing across the edge of the Low Forest though, I was tired and starting to become frustrated. It felt as though I'd traveled an eternity since I'd left home.

The guys remained close to Nyalla, but she'd moved to the back once out of the mountains.

Gwen was leading, her knowledge of the Low Forest superior to ours.

I kept a close eye on Nyalla. To be fair, if she'd was planning to do anything Will or Sel would have been the first ones to notice, given the way they hung on her every word.

GWEN WAS happy to be back in her element, as were the wolves, and conversation was minimal as they loped across the rolling prairie grass with contentment. Gwen found a sheltered grove of trees for our resting spot and I built the shelter the way Loglan had taught me. I was pleased with how much quicker I was able to complete it and was proud my skills as a traveler had come a long way.

"Rhin, do you want to take first watch? Seeing as how you built the shelter?" Gwen raised an eyebrow as she prodded the fire.

"Sure." I was tired but grateful for the offer when I remembered first and last watch were the most coveted because they allowed the longest stretch of sleep.

"I can take second if you'd like," Nyalla offered.

I plastered a fake smile on my face as the key protested

with a small burst of warmth. "Sure. I can wake you, no problem."

But it totally was a problem. I knew as long as I had my suspicions, it would be difficult to sleep well during her watch.

If it wasn't for the fact I was exhausted every night, I wouldn't have been sleeping as well as I had. Each night when we stopped, I worried I'd wake to find our camp overrun with ur'gel, or she'd murder everybody during her watch. But there was no way to voice my concern without drawing Will's objection, and potentially alienating the others as well.

As the others faded into dreams, I stared at the fire, occasionally poking it, or adding another log to keep it going. We usually allowed it to burn down a little during the night, but kept it going strong enough for the glow to detract the other forest animals.

At night, our best defense was the wolves, who slept nearby. When I remembered them, I felt a little better. Surely, they wouldn't be fooled by Nyalla and would protect us if Nyalla tried to harm us while we were asleep.

When I went to wake her for her turn, the key thrummed with the same steady warmth it always did when I was near her. But this time, it seemed confused, and left me with an odd chill when it suddenly went cool.

Nyalla blinked, then yawned and looked at me. I wasn't sure if it was my imagination or if her eyes were a different color. It must be a trick of the light. Or was it? Forcing myself to act normally, I smiled insincerely down at her.

"It's your turn, Nyalla." I yawned but caught it in my throat when she sat up and shook her head.

"When will you ever get it straight?" Her voice sweeter and higher than usual. My heart sank even before she said anything else.

"My name is Y'serra. Y-saaaa-rah. Get it straight." She rolled her eyes and stood up, stomping over to the fire and sitting next to it.

Completely dumbfounded, I stood where I was for a moment before following her.

She raised an eyebrow. When I still didn't speak, she prompted me. "Yes? What is it?"

She looked into the dark night, squinting into the distance. I followed her gaze into the well-lit night and saw nothing but grassland and trees. She shook her head and held a hand up demandingly. "What? Has something happened? Or are you just going to stand there and stare at me?"

Cautiously, I sat down perpendicular to where she was so I could see her face, but far enough away so she couldn't easily grab me. Everything about her looked the same as it had before she'd fallen asleep, but now I was looking for them, subtle changes were there.

As the light from the fire lit her face with a soft glow, I could see her eyes were a slightly different shade. The biggest change was her voice, exactly how she'd sounded the last time, when she'd woken up and told us her name was Y'serra.

"Why are you here?" I cut through any pleasantries and right to the heart of the matter. "What is your connection to Nyalla?"

Y'serra shrugged. "Let's just say sometimes we share a body." She seemed unperturbed by my tone even though I was trying to be rude.

"So, when can I expect you to betray us? I mean, that's who you are after all, isn't it? The Great Betrayer?"

Y'serra shook her head. "I'm not the one who will betray you. I'm not the bad guy here. Nyalla is."

I narrowed my eyes. I didn't trust her any more than I trusted Nyalla, especially since seeing her nocturnal persona emerge, but it instantly dawned on me Y'serra might be telling me the truth. The key cooled, as if waiting to see what I'd do next.

"I don't understand. What do you mean, Nyalla is the bad guy?"

She sighed, looking into the moonlit grasslands. This time I kept my gaze firmly trained on her, not trusting her not to pull something if I looked away.

"Nyalla is the one who means to betray you."

She looked into my eyes, and I thought I caught the faintest hint of worry. The key was still pulsing, but this time, I felt as if it was in agreement instead of in warning. I wished it could tell what it wanted me to do.

"How will she betray us? Is this about the Heart Stone?"

Y'serra agreed, picking her words carefully as she answered. "Yes. If Nyalla knows where the Heart Stone is, whoever is there is in danger of attack by ur'gel when she decides to take it for herself. There's no way Nyalla will ever allow you to take the stone back to the Library without doing everything she can to ensure it falls into her own hands instead."

As I watched Y'serra, I bit the inside of my cheek. While she may have vehemently denied she was the betrayer, I knew it didn't matter. While only the second time I'd seen her, she had just confirmed my suspicions.

Whether it was Nyalla or Y'serra who wasn't trustworthy, whoever was in her body would eventually betray us. Clearly, we were already in danger from having her with us. Not only did she likely know everything Will did, but if we did find the stone, she would have instant access.

How could I convince the others now? They'd all fallen under her spell. Could this be the reason why there had been so many ur'gel attacks in the desert? If Nyalla was commanding them, she'd quite literally been herding us in the direction she wanted us to go. Logically, she was also the reason we hadn't been attacked so far, which could change the second we found the stone.

I needed to figure out a plan to stop her, with or without the assistance of my friends.

I stared into the dark, unable to sleep as Y'serra watched

the fire. It wasn't until she woke Gwen I was finally able to relax enough to close my eyes. I was certain the only reason we hadn't yet been betrayed was because we hadn't found the stone, but it was only a matter of time.

When that time came, I needed to be ready.

CHAPTER 24

All the next day, I waited, biding my time. As I had expected, the next time I spoke with Nyalla-Y'serra, she was again in her previous persona of the helpful guide. No one else knew what I'd seen during the night and I'd been so uncertain what to do I'd done nothing, fearing ridicule or worse, betrayal by my friends if I shared my concerns.

I wondered if I was paranoid simply because of the continual pulsing of the key. It had kept me on edge the entire night, making it hard to fall back to sleep. Or was it because I truly had something to worry about? Regardless of the reason why, I knew it would be difficult to tell them.

Not only was I certain Will would choose to stand by Nyalla, as infatuated as he seemed, but I was almost a certain Sel would as well.

Gwen had initially seemed to harbor the same concerns as I did, but I was no longer sure I could count on her in this matter. Assuming I could even get her alone long enough to share my worries without being overheard by the others.

I said nothing as we traveled through the grassy areas of the Low Forest toward the Western March. As we set up camp when the sun was setting, I had an idea. Eager to see if it had any merit, I took a chance and volunteered to head out to try my hand at hunting.

Gwen looked at me skeptically after I'd made my announcement. "Are you sure? I mean," she grimaced, clearly recalling our last hunting trip, "you've only done it once before, and I was with you, as well as the wolves."

I nodded. "I'm sure. Besides, I seem to remember single-handedly taking down a deer. Not too bad for my first time."

She squinted one eye, still looking at me dubiously. "True, but it was driven to you because the wolves flushed it out of the trees. Not to mention as cool as it was, it was mostly luck which allowed you to succeed."

While I agreed with her, I pretended to be upset. "Are you saying you don't think I can?"

I felt guilty about what I was doing, but I needed time alone without making anyone suspicious. I could feel Nyalla's eyes on me, so I assumed a hurt expression and as I'd hoped, Gwen's face fell.

"Rhin, I didn't I mean … I'm so sorry! Of course, you can. I'm only worried about your safety."

I pushed aside my doubts. I wanted to explain, but for now there were too many other pairs of ears and not enough certainty for me to chance it. I shrugged and looked down to avoid her reading something on my face I didn't want her to see.

"I want to prove to myself I can do this without anyone helping me." I shrugged, slowly looking up with a half-smile.

Her worried expression eased somewhat, followed by a widening of her eyes and a smile. For a moment I thought she'd offer to come with me, and I wasn't sure how to handle it if she did. Especially since I wasn't keen to be on my own and always wanted her at my side.

"I know! If you want to prove you can hunt without my help, why don't you take the wolves? True, it's not completely alone, but the idea of you without any backup at all will make me worry until you get back. What about an ur'gel attack, or if you get injured? This way you're still hunting alone, mostly, but you have help if you need it."

I couldn't help but smile at the hope on her face. It was a good solution, and one I hadn't considered. "Perfect. Do you think they'll stay with me? I mean, they are your bonded wolves, after all."

She nodded to me as she called them over. She knelt, conversing with them in a way I couldn't understand, and when she stood up seemed pleased.

"We've reached an agreement. Swift doesn't want to leave us unprotected, so Damio will stay at the campsite with me while he and Kiya will go with you."

"Thanks. I'm happy to accept. I'll try not to be too long. I want to be back at the campsite before twilight."

"I'm holding you to that. If I don't hear from you, expect me to come looking." Her eyes narrowed with warning.

I nodded in agreement and she pulled me into her arms. We embraced quickly under the watchful eyes of the others, then I set out with my satchel across my chest and Swift and Kiya close at my sides.

I waited until we were far enough away, maybe a ten-fifteen-minute walk from the camp, before I found a sheltered area to sit. Swift and Kiya had remained at my side, not roaming the way they would usually. Whatever she'd told them had obviously impressed protecting me as their first and most important duty.

They watched as I sat, heads cocked to the side. I smiled at their confused whines, knowing they hadn't expected this. Looking around to make sure no one had followed to hear me I spoke to them, even though I felt foolish.

"I didn't actually want to go hunting, Swift. But thank you for coming. You too, Kiya." I hoped they could feel my gratitude. "The real reason I came out here alone was because I don't trust Nyalla. And I'm not sure if I can tell the others because they don't appear to share my suspicions about her."

I shrugged, feeling foolish even though the wolves had sat attentively on their haunches as I spoke. It was nice to have someone listen without interrupting. I figured I may as well keep telling them. It had been weighing on me heavily and letting it out felt good.

"I plan to use my book to ask Jarid for help. Do you remember him? He's back at the Library. He told me he'd help me if I needed anything right before we left. Well, during the trip we found out Nyalla has another person inside her. Or perhaps she's just pretending to be Nyalla. Twice now, I've seen her appear as another woman, someone she says is Y'serra."

I looked at Swift. His eyes were so wise I felt he understood what I was saying.

"Y'serra is a name I haven't seen or heard mention of outside of texts I've read about the Dark War. Another name Y'serra is known by is the Great Betrayer, because she was Onen Suun's true love— until she left him to join Dag'draath to fight on the side of darkness. I know how crazy it sounds, which is why I need more proof. Either proof, or I have to wait until she outs herself in front of everyone. So far neither Nyalla, nor Y'serra, have done anything suspicious."

Both wolves watched with patient eyes, and when Swift placed his head on my shoulder, I leaned into his warmth. His fur smelled of pine and sunshine, and some of my tension eased.

"I don't know what to do. The passage about her was light on details, but the key to the Library seems to be warning me about her constantly."

I paused to pull the top of my shirt down enough the wolves could see it. It gave off a burst of warmth, almost as if it was speaking directly to the wolves. Swift nodded at it wisely and looked at me again.

"Could you help me? If you caught something, it would help with my cover. I will sit here and wait for Jarid to answer. I hope he can help get a message to the Western March so they can relocate the Heart Stone before Nyalla or Y'serra, whoever she is, doesn't get it first."

For moment, I felt dumb spilling out the entire story to the wolves. They still watched me attentively, but I was sure they hadn't understood a thing. Then, to my surprise, Kiya bobbed her head and darted into the trees.

Swift stayed with me, but nuzzled my satchel, as if pointing out my book.

A smile split my face as I realized what he was telling me. "Thanks, Swift."

I exhaled, quickly jotted a note to Jarid in the book then sat back to wait.

Silence had fallen in the small copse of trees I'd chosen to rest. I looked out into the dimming daylight. It was becoming a beautiful night, with the sunset painting the portion of the sky I could see in oranges, reds, and purples. When I looked down, writing appeared on the page before me.

It was messy, as if it had been written in haste. Even in the terse words I was able to sense his concern.

How is this possible? Your guide is the Great Betrayer? If you are correct, you need to hide the Heart Stone immediately. I cannot give you any details about its location you don't already know. The last documentation I was able to find about it in the Library showed it in Mahimānbita Sūrya, where you've already been.

If the stone truly is in the Western March now, it is possible it's already on the move. The only thing I can think of to help is tell you to attempt to contact Runa Thorl. She's a powerful dreamwalker who lives there. If you can find her, perhaps she can guide you or find it for you.

I can give you a spell to reach her, but it isn't an easy one. You must dreamwalk to let her know they are in danger. If you are correct about your guide, most likely she'll send an army of ur'gel after the stone. You must warn them to take the stone far away, and to mount their defenses.

I quickly replied.

What? How? I thought dreamwalking was something limited only to a few naturally born to it?

It felt like forever for the words to appear, but when they did, I almost dropped the book.

Generally, that's true. However, you still have the key to the Library. We know it has allowed you to do magic before. With your own innate magic, even as untrained as you are, the key may be able to help you succeed. Good luck.

I THANKED him for his help and when he sent the spell, I memorized it. I was relieved to see it required nothing other than reciting a few simple words and falling asleep. Of course, I knew the simplicity of a spell was no guarantee of success, but it buoyed my hopes.

It was immediately clear the spell would be harder than it appeared when I found it impossible to get to sleep.

Swift looked at me curiously, his intelligent eyes seeming to size up the situation faster than I could explain it. He approached again, snuggling up to lay beside my head. With no idea whether it was intentional or simply a byproduct of his soft, warm fur so close to me, within moments I began to feel drowsy.

As I drifted to sleep, I smiled. "Thanks, Swift. I don't know what I'd do without you. No wonder you're her favorite people."

Just before I faded off, I repeated the words written on the paper and concentrated on where I needed to go.

BLINKING, I opened my eyes. I was in a place I didn't recall being before. For moment I thought I was dreaming. When the realization the spell had worked sunk in, I felt like crowing with pride.

Now, I just needed to find Runa. I took a moment to size up my surroundings. It was true the scenery was of a rocky landscape, different than the soft grassy hills and scattered trees I'd been surrounded by when I'd fallen asleep, but I appeared now to also be in a strange city, standing right beside a small house. If I was lucky, Runa would be inside.

I took a deep breath, feeling strangely like myself even though I my body wasn't there. It was a weird dream, not dream, and I was both gratified at my success and terrified by it.

I walked with a halting gait to the house, knocking with a tentative rapping. When nothing happened, I pushed on it.

The door swung open beneath my hand easily. Entering with nervous steps, I wasn't sure if the usual etiquette applied to the dream state, or if it was acceptable for me to wander around a stranger's home looking for someone.

"Hello, Runa? My name is Rhin. I am a Librarian, originally from Cliff Castle in the Low Forest. The Library has chosen me to seek out artifacts in order to end the growing darkness. But I need your help. The Western March and all of its people are in danger."

The house remained eerily quiet, and no one answered my tentative call. The creak of the door opening behind me made me whirl around, my hand reflexively leaping to my throat and to the key resting underneath my shirt.

The person who had entered through the door opened was a tall human woman, with unusual eyes that seemed to see past reality into the mists beyond and a face much older than what her youth should have suggested.

"Runa? Are you Runa?"

The woman nodded, tilting her head to regard me with curiosity but not fear. Either I didn't appear frightening, or she was able to tell instantly I was dreamwalking.

"Yes, I am Runa. Why are you here?" She paused and looked me up and down before adding," I don't recall seeing an elf dreamwalk before. How did you manage to accomplish such a feat?"

I shrugged, not wanting to anger her but not sure what her question had to do with anything. "I'm a Librarian, from Abrecem Secer. I was given a spell and told I needed to find you."

Runa looked surprised, but a trickle of fear soon darkened her eyes. "Someone sent you to find me?"

I shook my head. "I need your help. Someone is coming to take the Heart Stone. Someone who was supposed to be long gone from this world, but now appears to be alive and well."

Runa waited silently. When I realized she wasn't going to respond, I sighed. "The Great Betrayer, Y'serra, is back and she wants it. She knows it was brought here, to the Western March, and I fear she'll stop at nothing to get it. You can't let her get it. Please, find it and bring it to the Library. It will be safe there."

Her eyes locked with mine. I could tell she believed me but before she could speak, the angry peals of alarms going off outside the house drowned her out. The same type of alarms I'd heard when we'd escaped the Oubliee.

The city was under attack.

Runa turned to leave, but before she did, she hesitated. With a firm jaw and determined eyes, she held her hand up in a gesture of honesty. "I will do what I can. I promise on my life, I will get the Heart Stone out of here if it's the last thing I do. It appears your warning has arrived too late but thank you for trying. Maybe we shall meet again."

As she hurried out, I was overcome by exhaustion and crumpled to the floor.

CHAPTER 25

The rasp of a sandpaper tongue returned me to my surroundings.

I opened my eyes to the vision of Swift, watching me with concern in his ice-blue eyes. When he saw I was awake, he moved back slightly to allow me to sit upright. As everything rushed back, I started to shake. It was as if he understood my feelings better than I did, and when the first hot tears scalded my cheeks, he was already there, providing support before I realized I needed it.

"I was too late, Swift. I found Runa, but they were already under attack."

I stood up, feeling my legs tremble slightly. Too little, too late to stop the death and destruction I knew would come in the wake of an ur'gel attack.

Runa promised she'd try to get the stone, but the odds of her making it out alive weren't favorable, let alone finding the Heart Stone during a melee as well.

Swift lent me strength as I rose and I hugged him around the neck, finally standing straight and tall. It was time to return to my friends. If Nyalla knew her minions were attacking the Western March in advance of our arrival, perhaps she didn't need us anymore. My breath caught as the thought crossed my mind.

What if she tried to kill them before I returned?

I bit my lip, glancing down at Swift. Our eyes met and he nodded slightly. Before I could speak, Kiya bounded into the clearing with a small rabbit in her mouth, appearing pleased with herself. Even though I was terrified for my friend's safety, I almost laughed at Swift's judgmental expression.

"Thank you, Kiya. It may be small, but it's something."

At my words of praise, Kiya seemed to smirk at Swift. If I hadn't known any better, the interplay between Kiya and Swift seemed to be almost fraternal. But my amusement was brief, and I turned, running back in the direction of the camp with the wolves at my heels. I was even more grateful I'd stayed nearby once the idea of Nyalla disposing of my friends had hit me.

My stomach twisting with worry, I returned to find a fire crackling cheerily in the near dark. Sel poked at it with a stick, as he would have any other night, and my stomach finally settled into its usual home. It was too late to keep the acid from burning an unpleasant ache into the middle of my abdomen, but at least my clenched stomach hadn't been a precursor to heartbreak.

He looked up as a twig broke under my foot and smiled, waving me over. I held up the lone rabbit Kiya had presented to me like she'd won a trophy and tried to look pleased.

He smiled again, but less broadly. "Umm, great? You were gone for hours. Not much out there, I guess." His words were mild, but his disappointment was obvious.

Nyalla joined us, smirking when she saw the rabbit. When she spoke, she smiled, but it didn't reach her eyes. "That's it? Well, I guess it's a good start. For a novice."

I bit my tongue instead of angrily telling them what I knew, forcing myself to shrug instead. "Well, it *was* only my second time. I could make a stew with it?"

Nyalla shook her head. "No, I'll go and find something else. I'm more comfortable finding game after dark, anyway."

I realized I hadn't seen the others and turned to Sel. "Where's everyone else?"

He waved his free hand in the direction of the camels. "Last I saw, Gwen was feeding the camels and Will was setting up the last of our sleeping gear. Damio was helping."

I nodded reluctantly, turning to frown at Nyalla. "Are you sure it's safe to go out after dark? I can go with you, if you'd like."

I had no intention of leaving my friends again but didn't want her to become suspicious. After all, everyone had objected when I'd tried to leave on my own and I knew it was the expected response.

Nyalla shook her head, giving me a cool, confident look. "No, I'll be faster and quieter alone. Don't worry about sending the wolves with me. I'll be more inconspicuous without them."

I waved as I watched Nyalla slip out of the campsite. Once she was out of sight, I looked at the rabbit and got to work.

By the time I'd done what I hoped was a decent job of draining the blood and skinning it, Gwen and Will had joined us at the campfire. Once the rabbit was roasting on a spit Gwen had rigged, she turned to me.

"What is it? I don't think I've ever seen an expression quite like that on your face. What happened when you were out there?"

I rubbed my forehead. How could I tell them what I'd seen without sounding crazy? When Swift bumped against my leg, I suddenly understood. I took a deep breath, exhaled, then took her hand.

"The real reason I left to hunt wasn't to practice my hunting skills."

She searched my eyes. Hers glinted a dark emerald in the

light of the campfire as she absently bit her lip. "What did you do?"

I sighed, this time, speaking loudly enough for the guys to hear.

"I needed to be alone to contact Jarid. You see, the other night when everyone was sleeping, Nyalla changed again." I paused as I looked at my friends, waiting for their reaction. When all I saw was confusion, I elaborated. "I spoke with her and asked if she meant us harm, but she told me it wasn't her we needed to watch out for, it was Nyalla."

Will exploded onto his feet, clenching his hands into tight fists. "No. It's not possible. She's been nothing but our savior. She's far too kind to ever hurt anyone."

"Is she though?"

Sel spoke so quietly and unexpectedly Will stopped, staring at him.

When Sel saw he had our undivided attention, he turned the rabbit over on the spit, before he spoke again. "Think about it. True, she's always kept us safe, but at the same time everything has gone just the tiniest bit wrong whenever we've tried something when she's been around. The ur'gel attacks, our escape, even when we were recaptured at Jaydraberg. Each time we've arrived, it's been too late for our mission to succeed."

Will sunk back down onto the rough log he'd been using as a chair and rested his elbows on his knees, clasping his palms together as though praying. "But how could she be responsible for any of those things? She was with us the whole time."

He shrugged. "Was she? There's been a few times where she's left for short periods. Not to mention it's hard to trust someone once they tell you someone evil may be inhabiting their body. Or have you forgotten that part? I couldn't. I wouldn't be surprised to get to the Western March and find we're too late and the stone is gone."

My face drained of color as he gave voice to my greatest fear.

Gwen noticed, placing a hand on my cheek.

"What is it? There's more, isn't there?"

I swallowed hard, reluctantly sharing what I'd seen. "I dreamwalked with a spell Jarid gave me. I've already been to the Western March and spoke with their dreamwalker, Runa Thorl. But I was too late. By the time I reached her, the city was under attack. They beat us there."

Gwen shook her head, her face ashen. "We're less than a day away. How?"

"Nyalla knows our every move. I don't have any idea what kind of powers Y'serra or Nyalla possess. For all I know, she could have been passing messages to someone at any point. For all I know, she can dreamwalk as well."

Sel nodded solemnly and when I looked at Will, I was sad for his transformation. While he still looked angry, much of his disbelief had shifted to pain.

He believed everything he was hearing, even though he didn't look like he wanted to. His mouth was pressed into a line and he was sitting with his left palm cradling his forehead. He stared into the fire, like a man who'd lost sight of a dream.

"Will? Are you okay?" I wasn't sure what else to say and remembered how horrible I'd felt when I thought I'd lost Gwen forever. Something told me he was feeling the same way now.

He forced a smile as his eyes met mine and I knew he believed me. He was on my side, no matter how he felt about Nyalla.

"Why didn't you say anything sooner?" Gwen tilted her head to the side with a mix of disappointment and confusion in her face.

"To be honest, I didn't know for certain until today. And I was worried you'd think I was crazy. Or worse, you'd chose to believe her over me. After what I saw in the Western March, I have no doubts left. We can't trust her. As long as the Great Betrayer is with us, we're all in danger. All this time, I thought Y'serra was the one we needed to watch, but I was so wrong. Nyalla is the one who's been our enemy this entire time."

Continue reading this series, Legends of the Fallen with book 9, Mind Ring

Grab the free prequel to the Legends of the Fallen series, Falling Suun here:
https://books2read.com/u/3R1ElD

Like the series Facebook page to stay up to date on all new releases
https://www.facebook.com/LegendsoftheFallen

ABOUT THE AUTHOR

J.A. Culican is a USA Today Bestselling author of the middle grade fantasy series Keeper of Dragons. Her first novel in the fictional series catapulted a trajectory of titles and awards, including top selling author on the USA Today bestsellers list and Amazon, and a rightfully earned spot as an international best seller. Additional accolades include Best Fantasy Book of 2016, Runner-up in Reality Bites Book Awards, and 1st place for Best Coming of Age Book from the Indie Book Awards.

J.A. Culican holds a master's degree in Special Education from Niagara University, in which she has been teaching special education for over 13 years. She is also the president of the autism awareness non-profit Puzzle Peace United. J.A. Culican resides in Southern New Jersey with her husband and four young children.

For more information about J.A. Culican, visit her website at: www.jaculican.com.

ABOUT THE AUTHOR

I'm a full-time worker bee, mother, and writer by the wee hours of the day. I would write all the time if I had my way, but alas, life and family come first!

Somewhere in the last few years I've managed to carve out just enough time to write the trilogy that has spawned it all, based on a recurring dream I've had since my teens.

I hope you enjoy this world as much as I do.

For more information about H.M. Gooden, visit her website at: https://www.hmgoodenauthor.com/

ACKNOWLEDGMENTS

Editor: Frankie Blooding
Cover Artist: Christian Bentulan
Formatting: Dragon Realm Press

www.ingramcontent.com/pod-product-compliance
Lightning Source LLC
Chambersburg PA
CBHW060549310726
48982CB00008B/1061/J

* 9 7 8 1 9 4 9 6 2 1 1 4 3 *